Alfred Hitchcock asks,
"WHO NEEDS TOADS?"

Of course, Hitchcock is familiar with the traditional forms of satanic sorcery—but he much prefers more elegant instruments of evil.

A lovely, diamond-ringed hand, for instance, dropping poison into the lobster bisque . . . an expensive revolver being pulled from a Mark Cross attaché case . . . a pair of Gucci loafers hurrying from the scene of a crime . . . a gleaming Porsche racing along blood-slick highways . . . a yacht sailing before the wind and leaving behind a wake of well-fed sharks. . . .

With ingredients like these, Hitchcock guarantees the most delicious deviltry he's ever had the perverse pleasure of concocting—

WITCHES' BREW

13 ever-twitching tales of terror by the masters

Witches' Brew

Alfred Hitchcock
Editor

A DELL BOOK

Published by
DELL PUBLISHING CO., INC.
1 Dag Hammarskjold Plaza
New York, N.Y. 10017

Dell ® TM 681510, Dell Publishing Co., Inc.

ISBN: 0-440-19613-2

Printed in the United States of America

Previous Dell Edition #9613
New Dell Edition
First printing—February 1978

ACKNOWLEDGEMENTS

"PREMONITION" by Charles Mergendahl—Copyright 1957 by H. S. D. Publications, Inc. Reprinted by permission of Harold Matson Company.

"A SHOT FROM THE DARK NIGHT" by Avram Davidson—Copyright 1960 by
H. S. D. Publications, Inc. Reprinted by permission of the author and
the author's agents, Scott Meredith Literary Agency, Inc.

"I HAD A HUNCH, AND . . ." by Talmage Powell—Copyright 1960 by
H. S. D. Publications, Inc. Reprinted by permission of the author and
the author's agents, Scott Meredith Literary Agency, Inc.

"A KILLING IN THE MARKET" by Robert Bloch—Copyright 1958 by H. S. D.
Publications, Inc. Reprinted by permission of Harry Altshuler.

"GONE AS BY MAGIC" by Richard Hardwick—Copyright 1960 by H. S. D.
Publications, Inc. Reprinted by permission of the author and the author's
agents, Scott Meredith Literary Agency, Inc.

"THE BIG BAJOOR" by Borden Deal—Copyright 1962 by H. S. D. Publications, Inc. Reprinted by permission of Harold Ober Associates, Inc.

"THE GENTLE MISS BLUEBEARD" by Nedra Tyre—Copyright 1959 by
H. S. D. Publications, Inc. Reprinted by permission of the author and
the author's agents, Scott Meredith Literary Agency, Inc.

"THE GUY THAT LAUGHS LAST" by Philip Tremont—Copyright 1960 by
H. S. D. Publications, Inc. Reprinted by permission of the author and
author's agents, Scott Meredith Literary Agency, Inc.

"DIET AND DIE" by Wenzell Brown—Copyright 1962 by H. S. D. Publications, Inc. Reprinted by permission of Margaret Christie.

"JUST FOR KICKS" by Richard Marsten—Copyright 1958 by H. S. D. Publications, Inc. Reprinted by permission of the author and the author's
agents, Scott Meredith Literary Agency, Inc.

"PLEASE FORGIVE ME" by Henry Kane—Copyright 1959 by H. S. D. Publications, Inc. Reprinted by permission of the author and the author's
agents, Scott Meredith Literary Agency, Inc.

"A CRIME WORTHY OF ME" by Hal Dresner—Copyright 1961 by H. S. D.
Publications, Inc. Reprinted by permission of the author and the author's
agents, Scott Meredith Literary Agency, Inc.

"WHEN BUYING A FINE MURDER" by Jack Ritchie—Copyright 1960 by
H. S. D. Publications, Inc. Reprinted by permission of Larry Sternig
Agency.

CONTENTS

Introduction 6

Premonition Charles Mergendahl 9

A Shot from the Dark Night Avram Davidson 19

I Had a Hunch, And . . . Talmage Powell 31

A Killing in the Market Robert Bloch 43

Gone as by Magic Richard Hardwick 65

The Big Bajoor Borden Deal 80

The Gentle Miss Bluebeard Nedra Tyre 91

The Guy That Laughs Last Philip Tremont 104

Diet and Die Wenzell Brown 112

Just for Kicks Richard Marsten 121

Please Forgive Me Henry Kane 132

A Crime Worthy of Me Hal Dresner 150

When Buying a Fine Murder Jack Ritchie 169

Introduction

IT IS NOT OFTEN that I find myself with a sinister problem of major proportions.

I have a secretary who works for me on such projects as this volume, and she is an absolute terror. She is efficient, horribly efficient, and I find the situation most unnerving.

For the benefit of the uninitiated, a *secretary* is a bipedal, female mammal. In general, such a mammal is given to high heels, severely tailored business suits, and long hair—and this combines to form a regal manner. My *secretary*, unhappily, is given to flat heels, middy blouses, and short hair (I believe the coiffure is termed a "pixie"—heaven alone knows why!). Her bearing is decidedly unregal.

Now, there is nothing wrong with a secretary—either of the long-haired or short-haired variety—if she realizes that she is to provide an ordered existence for one's business life, but one must take offense when she begins to *order* one's existence.

I am known as a man of moderation, an admirer of womanhood, and a gentleman in the oldest and truest sense of the word—but even I must bridle at the sheer single-mindedness of being told not only *what* to do, but *when* to do each smallest thing.

I bridle.

I object.

I, ultimately, must revolt.

Let me cite as example the volume that you now hold in your hand. I enjoy such books. I do not mind the reading of several hundreds of thousands of words of stories; in fact, it is the most pleasant aspect of the undertaking.

However, my publishers insist that each volume contain an introduction by me, and such pieces, albeit short, take much labor and consume many hours of the most concentrated effort. Naturally, I must have absolute quiet for such work, and I must allow nothing to interfere with my thought processes during the time I am composing.

Because of the press of other matters, the introduction for this present book was very, very late; and my publishers in New York were howling for the manuscript.

I had planned to write it during a forthcoming weekend, which was free of commitments. I had thought to closet myself in my library on Saturday and then not emerge until the work was done.

Imagine my horror when, on Friday afternoon, my secretary informed me that she had made arrangements for me to appear on a television program in New York City over the weekend! She handed me my ticket, wished me a good trip, and left for a jolly time in Malibu.

It was impossible to work on the airplane, and my time in New York was so taken up with interviews that I had no extended period in which I was alone and could collect my thoughts. My publishers called several times, but I thought it wiser to defer talking with them until I had a manuscript to present.

At last, the terrible weekend was done with, and on the flight home to California I resolved that I would go to my office early the next morning and devote myself to my composition. Unhappily, I was so tired that I overslept and did not arrive at the office until almost noon.

I tried to make clear to my secretary that I had to cancel all appointments for the day in order to clear up this obligation. She smiled sweetly, and I thought she at last understood—and then she informed me that she had approved a schedule for me to film two openings for my television program. By the time this work was completed, Monday was finished. With sinking heart, I returned to my office. My secretary had left for home, and I checked the day's mail and phone messages. There were two calls listed from my publishers.

The next morning, during the drive to my office, the

car had two flat tires. The car was equipped with only one spare, which shows a certain shortsightedness on someone's part, I must say. I again arrived late, but vowed that nothing would prevent me from preparing the manuscript for immediate post to New York. I did not reckon with my secretary, for she had arranged script meetings for the entire day. I endeavored to change the appointments to the following day, but was told that one director was leaving that night to begin work on a Biblical drama in Europe, and that another was leaving to film a jungle epic in Africa. The day was again lost in frustration, and again there were two phone calls from my publishers—and a telegram: TIME SHORT BOOK ON PRESS PULLING OUT HAIR WHERE INTRODUCTION?

It is now Wednesday morning, and I find myself once more being thwarted by this fearsome woman—and I must revolt. I found a note on my engagement calendar for a ten-thirty appointment with a gentleman whom I do not know, to discuss I know not what. I therefore must take decisive action.

Fortunately, I am reminded of an interview once given by Robert Bloch, the able young man who wrote *Psycho*, a film which I trust you may have seen. Mr. Bloch also writes excellent short stories of terror and fantasy—one of which appears in this book, by the way—and when asked if he felt the type of story he wrote had any effect on him personally, he said "Oh, no, I have the heart of a small boy. . . . I keep it in a jar on my desk."

I believe I shall send my secretary out to look for a jar for me.

I do not know if she shall be successful in her quest, but enough for now of my little problems. I have a call in to my publishers to explain the situation to them, and before that call comes through, let me close, as always, by wishing you a shudderingly good time.

—*Alfred Hitchcock*

Premonition
Charles Mergendahl

MARTHA RICKER would be the next woman to be murdered. Not that anyone outside of Martha herself knew this for certain. Not her husband. Not the police. Perhaps not even the murderer himself. But Martha knew, for Martha had sensed her own doom in one of those "queer feelings" of hers that came frequently about many and varied things. The hurricane of '55, for example. She had sensed the presence of that hurricane a full week before the actual storm had swept down across the college campus and sent a huge oak crashing into the driveway. And the time that young physics instructor had run off with the president's private secretary—she'd felt that coming on, too, though others had laughed and paid little attention to what she'd said.

Now, of course, if they knew of her latest premonition, they would certainly laugh again. "The next woman to be murdered?" they'd say. "One of your queer feelings?" they'd say. And they'd snicker and remark nastily that these "queer feelings" of hers had been deliberately contrived in a foolish attempt to set herself apart from the other faculty wives. So they'd snicker, all right. And accordingly, Martha had told no one about her coming death. Not even Paul, her own husband. Not anyone at all.

But the killer *would* come. Tonight. Tomorrow. The day after. He'd come, all right. And she'd wait for him alone, as she waited now, staring out the window at the wet brown leaves, staring, too, down the long winding road around the campus—the road along which the man would walk, his feet moving slowly, his hands clenching and relaxing, clenching and relaxing, his eyes looking straight ahead, colorless perhaps, quite pale and white, the way a paranoiac's eyes always looked in those dreadful psychology books of Paul's.

But the road was empty, and after a long time Martha pulled her eyes away with some reluctance and moved into the kitchen, where she made a pot of strong coffee and spilled it because of her blunt, clumsy fingers. It was odd, really, how unafraid she was now. Somehow, even from the beginning, even after the second woman had been strangled and even after the third, she had never been really afraid, horribly, agonizingly afraid. "I suppose it's a kind of resignation to doom," she had told herself. "After all, I *should* be frightened, since even the police wouldn't help me. And really I can't blame them. After all, they can't send an officer to every house where someone 'feels' the man will probably come next. So here I'm going to be this maniac's fourth victim. . . . Nothing I can do at all."

The black coffee was followed by a cigarette. Then Martha returned to Paul's study window and her endless surveillance of the street. In a way she was glad that Paul was busy with his classes during these shortening fall days, because, like all the others, he only laughed at her premonitions. In fact, he laughed at everything about her now, her looks, her chatter, her temperament, her ideas—everything about her because he no longer cared. They lived together. They spoke words and made gestures. But none of it meant anything. He no longer cared.

So it was almost good to sit here quietly alone. She could watch the road and wait, with a strange anticipation, for the maniac's slouching figure; she could feel the slow, helpless fear that would finally come and cling to her body like wet, smothering fog. And she could know, regardless of pain and the certainty of death, that she had been right after all, and that when her limp body was finally found, one of Paul's neckties pulled tight around her throat, then Paul would be sad, perhaps relieved a little with her death, but awed and sad all the same when he read that explanatory note that she'd already prepared and tucked inside her desk. "She knew it would happen," Paul would say dumbly to the police. "She knew it all the time, and she knew I wouldn't believe her. No one would believe her. But she knew it all the time." And perhaps, in that moment of discovery, perhaps he would think a bit more seriously of his dead and twisted wife.

Now the darkness had come, slowly, creeping in over the campus like a black, noiseless cat. The wet leaves shone black and yellow in the street lights. Martha's cigarette glowed bright and faded, then moved in quick, jerky circles as she extended her shaking hand to tap an ash in a tray on the windowsill. Her breath clouded the pane, and her anxious face was pressed quite flat and cold against the glass.

The cigarette burned down to scorch her fingers, and still her eyes did not move. They stared unblinking into the deepening night, and her entire body waited expectantly until the figure finally appeared, as she'd known it would, slow and heavy, its legs moving out in short, determined strides, its head bent down, its black form growing larger as it advanced unswervingly up the road.

It was rather odd, the detached, curious way Martha watched the approaching silhouette. Once, in childhood, she had coasted down a long white hill, unable to steer the sled properly. There'd been a tree before her, and she'd watched it growing larger with an awesome calm, completely unafraid until that last final second before the crash, when the scream had finally come and the blackness had followed close behind. And it was the same now. Very much the same. She supposed, as she watched the approaching figure, that the scream would come later— when the necktie was raised, when the man's pale eyes were close to her own, fixed deep inside her with the madness bright in their colorless pupils.

So Martha Ricker sat motionless. She smoked and snubbed the cigarette. She noticed that the man walked with a slight, almost imperceptible limp. He wore a dark felt hat, and his hands were thrust into the pockets of his coat. Sometimes he glanced up toward the window where she sat waiting, and sometimes he glanced furtively from side to side. But always he moved closer, until finally his heavy feet scraped on the cement walk, sounded loud on the wooden steps. The brass knocker creaked up and fell—twice—with a long silence following.

Martha rose slowly. The telephone was near on the hall table. She lifted it quickly in sudden panic as the knocking continued. And then suddenly the door was pushed open behind her and the man stood there in the doorway, his eyes focused hard on her hand as the panic gave way to resignation, and she replaced the receiver on the hook.

He was a rough, middle-aged man with the pale eyes she had expected, with a large spreading nose, and a mouth that was thin and set, and hardly moved when he spoke. "Your husband? Is he at home?"

"No."

"You just called him?"

"No."

"No?" He almost smiled. "Then if I could speak to you," he said. "Just for a minute." He closed the door and watched her face for a second in the gilt mirror that hung above the phone. "McCready, my name is. McCready." Then he moved on to the living room.

Martha followed. McCready remained standing, waiting for her to be seated. She slumped in a chair near the fireplace, liking the warmth of the dying coals against her back. The man drew out a pack of cigarettes. His movements were slow and meticulous. His hands were strong—with hard, corded veins that ran up under the cuffs of his shirt. "Smoke?"

"No, I—I just finished one."

"I suppose you're wondering what I want."

"No . . . Not exactly."

"What do you mean, 'Not exactly'?" He leaned forward suddenly, dropped his cigarette, snatched it up and thrust it between his tight, unmoving lips. "What do you mean?"

"I mean I—well, I—I know what you came for."

For a moment the man did not move. Then his voice cracked in a high, unexpected laugh. "Well—well, that makes it easier, doesn't it?" His pale eyes darted to her face. "Although you don't seem—well, frightened. You should be, you know."

"Yes, I—" And she waited then, waited for the deep

terror that was sure to come, and felt it beginning slowly in the very small of her back, a tiny spot of cold. "I knew," she went on softly. "I knew you'd come all the time. I knew there was no way to prevent it." She laughed a little wildly. "I suppose it sounds ridiculous, even to you. But I knew it all the time."

For a long moment neither of them spoke. McCready smoked and studied his nails and glanced quickly toward the door each time a car passed in the street outside. And Martha watched him. She looked into his colorless eyes; she looked at his hard, paranoic face; and she looked deep inside herself as well. She felt the tiny cold spot rise slowly up her back; she felt dampness on her forehead, a tiny, imperceptible trembling in her hands. It was the waiting, she thought then. That's what it was, certainly—the waiting. She was only just beginning to realize that it had actually happened. The man had actually come.

Still McCready did not move. A coal dropped in the fireplace, and after a moment the telephone jangled.

McCready raised his head. "I'd rather you didn't answer it." A warning, the words carefully pronounced.

Martha sat motionless. She ran her tongue around her lips, found them dry, wet them again. She tried to light a cigarette, but couldn't, threw down the crumpled pack, and gripped the sides of her chair with stubby, aching fingers.

"Don't be afraid. You mustn't be afraid." The voice was far away now, soft and low, almost caressing her as the hysteria rose steadily from her stomach to her chest, as her eyes bulged and the realization cracked in upon her mind—she, Martha Ricker, was about to die.

The man pulled quickly to his feet when Martha screamed. He paused, then moved slowly toward her, watching her convulsed and ashen face, a set smile along his mouth. But Martha did not wait for the touch of his outstretched hand. She swung desperately on her heel, and still shrieking hysterically, stumbled wildly up the stairs and into the bedroom, where she slammed the door and leaned back against it, breathing hard in short, painful gasps.

It was a long time before Martha Ricker moved. There

was no way, she knew, of locking the door. She waited, hearing the man's step on the stairs, hearing his voice call softly. She heard him retire once more to the living room, and she heard her own heart beating fast and painfully in her chest.

The calm was gone now. The dull acceptance gone completely. And there was only one thought, only one desire—to escape, above all else to escape.

She started for the window, raised it, then cut off her own scream with a hot, trembling hand. A scream would bring him immediately. She could not scream. She mustn't scream. She couldn't climb out the window either; there was nothing on which to hold. But there was something else—the neckties. Paul's neckties. The man always used neckties—the husband's neckties. It was clever of her, really very clever to think of it now. And she was giggling to herself when she crossed the room, opened the closet door, dragged out Paul's neckties, and buried them deep under his shirts in the dresser drawer.

Then she staggered to the chaise longue in the darkness of the room. She clenched her fists and felt the uncontrollable trembling of her body. She listened and heard nothing. What was the man doing? She prayed he would go away. She prayed for Paul to come home. Funny about that. And she laughed hysterically with the ironic humor of the thought. She had never prayed for Paul to come home before. It was funny, too, that the possibility of Paul's fighting for her, risking his life for her, perhaps even dying for her, had never occurred to her until this exact moment.

Then, for a passing second, shuddering violently there on the chaise longue in her neat and darkened bedroom, Martha Ricker had quick, flashing glimpses of her husband, of herself, and what they had been to one another. How little she had trusted Paul really, not to want him with her until now, when it was so very, very late. How little she had believed in his understanding not to have told him about this "queer feeling" of hers a long time before, given him a chance to comfort her, call the police, even laugh at her if he chose. She had not given Paul a fair chance, really, and now she would die because of her own unfairness.

Her mind raced, exploded, went black, struggled desperately to concentrate. Her ears ached for the tiniest comforting sound. Downstairs there was only silence. Yet she knew that McCready was still there, still sitting before the fireplace, studying his knotted hands, waiting patiently for her to come down, wondering, perhaps, whether the game had gone on far enough, whether or not it was time for him to rise and walk into the hall, climb the stairs, enter her room, and get it over with once and for all.

Paul's neckties, though, were hidden away. It was small comfort. But it was something. It was something. And Martha giggled once more, let the giggle go on until it had become a laugh going steadily higher. The laugh broke finally in wild hysteria. She clutched the arms of the chaise longue and felt her entire body shaking with the laughter she could not control. She felt herself crying, trembling, forcing the laughter on, trying not to hear the footsteps that would come slowly, one at a time, creaking on the stairs.

And then, with a suddenness that startled even herself, Martha Ricker broke the hysteria off and sat quietly once more, tense, her ears strained for the most welcomed sound she could ever hope to hear. Paul was coming up the walk. She could tell by the way his feet scuffled in the leaves, by the thump of his heavy brogans on the porch stairs. The front door opened with the sure slow click she had heard so many times before, and then Paul's voice came muffled from the hallway.

"Martha. . . ! Martha. . . ! Are you upstairs, Martha?"

She started to answer, then held back the cry of relief and waited, praying that Paul would not go into the living room, closing her eyes and trying to speak to him with her thoughts, trying to warn him, to bring him safely up the stairs. It seemed hours before his footsteps finally sounded. And still Martha did not move. She rested wearily, with the weakness of great relief pushing her body into the chaise longue. And when the door finally swung in and Paul's tall, rather stooped figure appeared in the doorway, she could find no strength for words.

Paul stood motionless, peering about in the darkened room. "Are you there?" he said finally. "Are you there, Martha?"

"Yes. Yes, I'm here."

"In the dark? I'll get the light. I'll—"

"No, Paul!" Her urgent voice stopped his hand on the wall switch. "Shut the door, Paul!"

He turned back to her, frowned, shrugged, shut the door, and started taking off his coat and tie. Martha watched him dumbly, drinking in his comforting presence with her wide, frightened eyes. She wanted to say it calmly, to explain McCready in clear, definite words, so that Paul could think accurately of the right course of action, so there would be no danger for either of them.

"I'm sorry I won't be here for dinner." Paul's back was to her. He had changed his shirt and was buttoning it slowly, beginning at the bottom. "I'm going to be quite late. So don't wait up."

"Not here for dinner, Paul?"

"No. A meeting."

"What meeting, Paul? There's no meeting tonight." And suddenly she pulled to her feet and suddenly she had forgotten the man downstairs. She'd caught a glimpse of Paul's face, taut and different, and she knew then. "You're lying to me, Paul. It's a woman, isn't it? It's somebody else. Isn't that so?"

But Paul paid no attention. He opened the closet door, groped for his neckties, could not find them, and turned back slowly to face her. "All right, what have you done with my ties?"

"Paul, I—They're in the drawer. The second drawer." She was laughing again, stumbling about the room, talking on and on in a jabber of meaningless words. "You see I had to hide them, Paul. It was very clever of me, don't you think? And he could never find them and it was very clever of me, wasn't it, Paul?" She stopped and watched him move to the drawer where she'd hidden the ties. And McCready came back to her mind and she knew then that this, now, was the final test of Paul's love and courage. Now, in this moment, if Paul would fight for her very life—

unconsciously, because she was in danger and because he loved her—then everything else, this other woman, all the long dreadful months before, everything would be forgotten, washed away by this one act of self-sacrifice and strength. She saw her husband reach into the drawer, his back stooped, his shirt very white in the darkened room. Then she spoke, calmly now for the first time since it all began. "Paul . . ."

"Yes?"

"Downstairs, Paul. In the living room. That man. He's down there in the living room."

"That man?" Paul turned slowly to stare at her. "What man?"

"That maniac. The murderer. He came over an hour ago. I knew he was coming. You know my premonitions, Paul. Well, I knew it all the time, and I even wrote you a note about it. And he came, just like I knew he would, and now he's down there, just waiting, Paul—just waiting."

"You're crazy, Martha."

"No, Paul, he is."

"What did he say?" humoring her, not believing her.

"He asked if you were home and I said no and he came in then. He just sat there and played with me like a cat. Just like a cat with a mouse. But you'll save me, Paul. You will, won't you, Paul? You will, won't you?" The words came faster, repeated again and again in the dark, quiet room. She was pleading now, begging now, pleading for protection and love and courage and belief. She moved slowly toward her husband, crying his name, talking senselessly, until finally she was close to him, looking up at his face, and then the door opened slowly behind him and she saw McCready in the doorway.

The light from the hall made a perfect triangle on the floor. It touched Paul's face and eyes as he turned to meet the danger. He cried out, and then McCready moved and the two men came together. There was solid, resounding blows, grunts of pain, and muttered curses that seemed to hang there over the struggling figures. But in a moment it was over. A strong, comforting arm was around her shoulder, and finally her own voice came back again, saying, "You see, I knew. My queer feeling. I knew he'd come for me. I knew he would, I knew he would," until finally her voice died and she was silent, conscious of the sharp point of McCready's police badge against her breast.

Paul lay quite motionless on the floor. The necktie was still clutched tight between his fingers. His eyes, as his senses came struggling back, opened slowly. They were quite far away, like the eyes in those psychology books of his, a little pale, Martha thought absently, with the pupils entirely white.

A Shot from the Dark Night
Avram Davidson

IN A COUNTY SEAT in that part of our country where "evening" begins at 12 noon, a "poke" is not a nudge but a small bag, and fireworks are shot off on the 25th of December, there is a large wooden building, more or less square and painted white, that bears this sign across its front:

JAMES CALVIN "JAYSEY" WILLIAM
CASH AND CARRY GROCERIES

William also owns the larger of the two cotton gins, an automobile agency, the only decent hotel, the big produce place by the railroad, and quite a number of other commercial interests and pieces of real estate. But it would be wrong to jump to conclusions and say that he "owns the town." The town is owned by the people who live in it and they are a proud and independent people. They elected James Calvin William to be their mayor, on several occasions, and are intending to elect him either to sit in the State Senate or to head the County Court—whichever he wants, not because so many of them work for him, but because they like and respect him. No one begrudges him his success. He deserves it, they feel, because he has worked hard for it.

Mr. William's home is within easy walking distance of his office, and he has a wife and two daughters and a cook, all of whom would gladly fix him a cup of coffee in the middle of the forenoon. However, it is his custom to go across the street to Turbyfull's Café, and have his coffee. He paused at the door, this particular morning, to talk to the proprietor. When at last he swung up on the stool, the man behind the counter had his coffee poured. William tasted it and it was just the way he liked it.

"I see they told you about my tastes," he said to the counterman.

"Yessir, Mister Jaysey, they done tole me," the man said, smiling a bit. He had a red, battered face; his smile was rather awry.

A thin man with a shrewd face and gray hair seated himself next to William. "Made up your mind, yet, Jaysey?" he asked. "Is it going to be 'Senator' William, or 'Judge' William?" This was the sheriff, Tom Wheeler, a good man, but inclined to talk too much.

"You'll be the first to know. . . ." William sipped his coffee. "Only thing is, I don't know I care so much for being away at the State Capital. I'm just an old country boy."

The sheriff ordered sweet milk and pie. "Why, the legislature don't meet but once in two years," he pointed out, and they talked the matter over until they were done eating and drinking.

At the door William paused, said to Wheeler and Turbyfull, "Who's the new counterman? Have I seen him before? Seems like I have."

They shook their heads. At the other end of the café, where he was cutting cheese, the counterman began to sing:

"There's an Eye up on high, watching you—
Ohwatchin' ev-er-a theng that you do—"

The men smiled. Turbyfull rubbed his heavy chin as he said, "In my opinion he's just a little bit simple. But he does his work good. Name's Jemmy. Holiness preacher brought him around yesterday."

William nodded. "Sounds like a real Holiness-type hymn. Bye, now."

Crossing the street he still felt he might have seen the man before.

Mr. Jaysey—as just about everyone, including his wife, called him—was not a native of the city (town, really) of Calhoun. He had arrived there about thirty years earlier from another part of the state with $5,000. He had bought a tractor franchise and a small farm. The farmers had still tended to stick to mules, but the success Jaysey William had with the farm had persuaded many of them to try tractors. He had never really lost ground, although during the depression years, for a while, he'd been hard put to it just to hold his own.

But that was all in the past, and he seldom talked about the past. All that the people of Calhoun knew about his early life was that he had been raised on a farm and had been in the First World War, though it had ended before he went overseas. On Confederate Memorial Day he wore the uniform of the local veterans' post in the parade. His only kin, a brother, had died a few years ago, and he had gone to the funeral. But he seldom left the county.

And each morning when he went to the café for his coffee, he felt a faint but insistent stirring of memory when he looked at the counterman, or heard him singing:

"The Lord, He is my shep-herd, I shall in peace abide.
He leads me to green pastures, and where still wa-ters hide."

Jemmy smiled his crooked smile as he fixed the coffee. "Your two gals, Mr. William," he said, "they looked might sweet and pretty when they taken the bus over to Three Springs this morning. They must be right proud of their daddy, he fixen to git the nomination, an all."

Jaysey had made up his mind; he would run for County Judge. After all—his friends told him, only half-jokingly—Harry Truman had been a county judge before becoming senator—to say nothing of achieving a somewhat higher office.

"I'm right proud of them," Jaysey said smiling. Once again he studied the counterman, who lowered his gaze bashfully. "You ever do any boxing, Jemmy?"

Jemmy cleared his throat, but the question was answered by Sheriff Wheeler, who had put down his glass of sweet milk.

"Them marks on his face," Wheeler said, "they wasn't made by no regular boxers. They was made by the guards down at the State Prison, wasn't they?"

The counterman nodded. His smile didn't change. "I thought I was a hard man in them days," he said. "But they was harder." He chuckled, as if someone had played a good joke on him.

The sheriff went on, "Jemmy was pardoned a few years back by old Governor T. I. Anstruther, for helping put out that big fire in the prison—"

Jaysey nodded. "I remember that, now, that big fire," he said.

"—and for pulling out three guards, what had passed out from smoke."

William continued to nod as the story unfolded. "I figured your face looked familiar," he finally said to Jemmy. "Guess I must've seen it in the papers that time."

"I was pretty wild when I was young," the ex-prisoner said, indifferently. Then something seemed to kindle in his eyes. "Maybe if I'd settled down then and married, maybe I'd have a right nice family of my own, by now— like y'all's, Mr. Jaysey."

Their eyes met. The counterman went on, not lowering his eyes "Of course, if I *had* married and *then* got into trouble, my children'd be ashamed of me. . . . Your children, now, Mr. Jaysey, they ain't got nothing to be ashamed of *you* for."

Outside, moved by a curiosity he couldn't altogether account for, Mr. Jaysey William asked the sheriff, "Why was he sent to prison, d'you know, Tom?"

The sheriff considered. "He tried to break out, he told me that. Naturally, he got some more time tacked on. . . . You mean originally? I b'lieve he shot somebody in a incident of some kind." He turned to William. "Wasn't you originally from Crookshank County?" William nodded. "Well, that's where it happened. Early twenties. His full name was—He's got same first name as you—James Buxton's his name. Ever hear of him?"

Miz Lizzy, as everyone called Jaysey's wife, had never forbade her husband to keep a bottle in the house.

"I want him to do at least part of his drinking where I can see it," was her explanation. Not that her husband did much drinking, at home or elsewhere. But Miz Lizzy was partial to exaggerate a bit. Tonight, as usual, the man of the house had a glass of whiskey and water about an hour before going-to-bed-time. He sat in his chair and drank it slowly.

Crookshank County. Farming country? Why, the soil was wearing thin, washing away in the rains. Timbering country? The timber was almost all cut, none had been replanted. It was a poor place. Those were poor times. James Buxton? Yes, William remembered him. Buxton had robbed the payroll of a state road project—one of few payrolls there were around then. He had been pursued and had shot one of the pursuers—not fatally. He then disappeared, and then rumors arose and flourished. Rumor credited him with having a gang, with planning raids on the local banks, with intending further depredations—one, for instance, on the only timber outfit still operating. All of these rumors turned out later to be false, but they did their work: rewards totaling $5,000 were offered for Buxton's capture and conviction. And the man who had collected the reward money, it so happened, was named James C. William.

Jaysey finished his glass of "toddy" and then mixed himself another, this one with less water. Thirty years had passed, no one hereabouts had ever mentioned the Buxton case to him before. No one had known about the affair, for it had occurred in a distant part of the state. No one knew that the foundation of Jaysey William's good fortune had been the money he collected by turning in Buxton. But there was the danger, now, the threat, that they soon might know.

Jaysey tried to recall the features of the young man of thirty years ago, to compare them with those of the counterman at Turbyfull's Café, but all that his memory could tell him was that he had seen the man before. When had he thought about James Buxton last? He couldn't recall this either. For it wasn't the case that he had been haunted by his conscience. He had collected the money; he had come to Calhoun with it; he had worked hard, married, raised a family—he had been too busy to dwell upon the past.

"Your two gals . . . they must be right proud of their daddy. . . ." That was what Buxton had said. *"Your chil-*

dren, now, Mr. Jaysey, they ain't got nothing to be ashamed of you for." How peculiar his eyes had looked when he said these things, William thought, and, thinking, he grew cold and sick with fear.

What was in Buxton's mind? Why had he come here, out of all the places in the state? It was no accident, that was for sure. What did he plan? Did he intend to ask money? Blackmail—was that it? Compensation for the years in prison, for the beatings, for the brutal life behind bars, in irons, years and years? Or would his reprisal take a more direct form? Violence. A shot from the dark night. And then something else occurred to Jaysey and his fingers quivered around the glass.

Buxton had mentioned his daughters—twice he'd mentioned them. Was *that* the way he'd chosen? And if it was, what could Jaysey do? And what could he do in any case? Tell the sheriff. Ask for the protection of the law. He got up from his chair. And immediately sat down again.

For if he spoke to the sheriff, he would have to tell the sheriff everything. Buxton wasn't on parole; he'd been pardoned. The man had made no overt threat. He was breaking no law. The sheriff would say, his tone surprised, "But I don't understand, Jaysey. Why should the man want to harm you or your daughters?"

Because thirty years ago, he'd have to say, I talked to the sheriff of Crookshank County as I'm talking to you, and I told him that James Buxton was hiding out in his uncle's barn. Thereupon Sheriff Lowestoft went with three deputies and took Buxton without a fight and he was tried and convicted and I collected the $5,000 which was mine by right of law.

If he told that to Tom Wheeler, he would have the protection he needed. His fear would be over. And so would his political career. And so would his life as the leading citizen of the town.

For Jaysey knew the people among whom he lived. No one would charge him to his face; no one would jeer at him or spit at him. But neither would they shake his hand or smile or stop to talk with him or eat his bread or ask his counsel. And certainly they would never vote for him.

He could hear them talking to one another, he knew what they would say.

James Calvin William could commit murder, could be taken in adultery; and there would be either forgiveness or an absence of condemnation.

Well, I reckon we're all sinners when you come right down to it.

But when it was known that he had collected a reward by informing, there would be no forgiveness. There couldn't be.

I ain't much, that's for sure, but I never betrayed my fellowman for money.

But all this fled from Jaysey's mind when he looked from his glass to the clock. He called to his wife—she always went in the kitchen at this time and made herself a cup of hot sweet milk, which she sipped while reading her nightly chapter from the Bible.

"Lizzy!" he called. "Where are the girls? How come they aren't back now?"

She said something he couldn't make out; then she came to the door. She was already in her night gown and her hair was in curlers. "—won't be over till near midnight," she said.

He put down his glass with a clatter, stood up. *"What* won't be over till midnight?"

She looked at him, drew up her mouth in a mock reproof, shook her head. She said, "I don't know where your *mind's* been since you come home, Jaysey. I believe you haven't taken in a word I've told you. Try to pay attention, and I'll tell you again: They've gone over to Three Springs to the Fall Frolic at the High School there, along with just about all the other boys and girls." She frowned at him. "I don't know why you're making that face. There's nothing to worry about. The Holiness preacher, Reverend Powell—"

At the words *the Holiness Preacher,* a train of alarm started in Jaysey's mind. Desperately he tried to follow it to its source. Why should he be frightened at the mention of the minister of the little unpainted wooden church near the cotton gin?

His wife went on, peering closely at him: "—he made so

much talk against allowing the girls to ride halfway across
the county at night in the boys' cars—said it wasn't safe
nor proper, they might some of them wind up in a jook-
joint or who knows where or what. The long and short of it
was, it was arranged they'd all go and come back in the
school bus. Well, I hear that some of the boys, they were
none too pleased, but—"

Jaysey's mind made the connection. He felt suddenly
very certain of something, and suddenly very afraid.
"Mother . . . who—who is driving the bus?" He knew and
his wife knew that the regular driver worked a short shift
from six to midnight at the local power plant.

"Why, what's wrong?" his wife asked, dismayed.

"Who's driving the bus!"

She shook her head, amazed, wet her lips. "Why, that
red-faced, sort of ordinary man. What's his name? The
Holiness preacher said—what *is* his name? *You* must
know: works in Turbyfull's. Face is sort of all marked
up . . ."

They stood around in the sheriff's office looking at each
other, then away from each other, then at the cluttered desk
with the pile of FBI flyers that the sheriff would never
throw away until a cancellation came through.

For the tenth time the sheriff began, "Well, I'll be—"
and for the tenth time, out of deference to Mrs. William
and the Reverend Powell, stopped himself, and continued,
"Well, I'll be darned."

The minister, a thin, rusty-looking man, with the tired
eyes of one who had wrestled long years with the devil
and was by no means sure of victory, repeated what he had
been saying again and again. "I wouldn't worry, Brother
William, Sister William. I know as I know anything that
Brother Buxton, whatever his past—"

Jaysey turned abruptly and went to the window, shaded
the pane against the glare of the light, peered out.

"—is a Christian man now. Oh, I wouldn't worry."

Lizzy said, "And besides, they're not alone. All those big
boys from the High School, they wouldn't let him do anything—they—"

Her husband swung around. "They mightn't get the

chance to stop him. He might," his face twisted at the thought, but he continued, "drive the bus off the road or something suddenly like that." Abruptly, he took his wife in his arms. "Oh, let him do what he wants to *me,* just so long as the girls aren't harmed!"

The minister said to the sheriff, "How long do you think it would take your deputies to overtake the bus and put one of them on it?"

Glancing at his watch, the sheriff started to speak. The phone rang. As he held the receiver and listened, his face tightened. He looked at the Williams, then looked quickly away—too quickly. He asked a question in a low voice. He said, "I'll start out right away."

They all stepped forward, began a babble of questions. "Let's get into my car," the sheriff said, shaking his head, and urging them out of the office. "I'll tell you what I know when we're on our way."

It was a dark night. Few other cars were on the road. The sheriff's car sped along.

Jaysey asked, calmer now than he had been for some time. "Did he say a girl? Or did he say girls?" His wife wept on his shoulder.

"Seemed like the man only mentioned a single girl," Sheriff Tom Wheeler said. "I didn't want to waste time asking him questions. Said the school bus had stopped by his gas station, said they were all yelling and screaming— that a girl'd been shot—the driver and one of the boys were tussling—and that's all."

The minister sighed deeply. "I still can't believe wrong of him."

"It's a judgment on me. I'm confident of that. My sins have found me out," William said, still calm. " 'Thou shalt not betray the fugitive'—doesn't the Bible say so? Oh, it's different with you, Tom. You got your job to do. But what I did, I just did for the money. It was my chance, I thought. I knew where he was hiding, knew I'd never get any other chance to find five thousand dollars. And once it was done, I forgot about him as if he'd never lived. Nor did I think of how he was living—rotting—"

Then they were there.

The students were gathered near the school bus, talking in low tones. One of the deputies from Three Springs stepped over as the new arrivals sprang from the car. "Well, it wasn't serious," he said. "It just grazed her shoulder. But she was shook up—hysterical almost, you might say, so—"

"Which one was it?" Jaysey demanded, his eyes searching the group.

"Was it Grace or Helen?" his wife's voice trembled.

The deputy's face wrinkled in puzzlement. "Why, the name as I got it, it was Nancy. Nancy Fanshaw. So, like I say, I sent her back to Three Springs in the doctor's car. . . . Inside, Sheriff. In the gas station." The sheriff went off with him. And so did the minister.

"Why, Daddy! What are you doing here?"

"Look, Grace. Mamma's here, too!"

And then Jaysey lost his calm and, as he hugged his daughters to him, he began to sob. His wife explained to the bewildered girls. The deputy reappeared and told Jaysey to come inside with him.

There Buxton was, in the tiny office, with the sheriff and the minister and two high school boys and the station owner, and now the deputy and Jaysey William. There was no particular expression on his battered face as he looked up and saw William. He just nodded slowly.

One of the boys was saying, "It never come to my mind to hurt her. Or to hurt anybody. I just took the gun there—" he pointed with his head. The weapon rested on a carton of flashlight bulbs. It was a very small revolver; it seemed almost like a toy. The mother-of-pearl inlay had broken from one side of the handle. "I took it just to shoot out the window—" a sudden thought struck him. "It belongs to my daddy. He finds out I took it, he'll whup me." And he hung his head and began to cry. The minister inched forward, and as he put his hand on the boy's shoulder and bent over to whisper into his ear, the other boy began to speak. The other boy was white and his lips were pale, but his eyes never left the boy who'd "just took the gun."

"If anything happens to Nancy—" he leaned forward. Jemmy Buxton raised an arm against the boy's chest to keep him back. "If she's hurt bad—"

Buxton said, "She ain't, though."

"—if she dies—"

"Shucks, she'll be eating six eggs for breakfast come morning," Buxton said.

"—if anything happens to Nancy, I'll kill you. I swear it: I'll kill you. If it takes me ten years—"

"I just wanted to scare them; I was just havin' some fun. I just took the gun and then the bus kind of hit a bump and it went off—"

"If I got to hang for it or lie my life in jail, I'll get you, if she's—"

Buxton turned so he was face to face with Nancy's boy-friend. He took him by the shoulders and dug in with his fingers. The young man winced. Slowly his eyes left the boy he was threatening and met Buxton's.

Buxton said: "Listen. You talk about jail. You talk about gettin' somebody. Listen. You never been in jail. I have. I been in two jails and three prison farms. I done wrong things when I wasn't much older than you, and it wasn't but right that I went to jail."

He paused. Outside there was the murmur of the students' voices, but in the tiny room no one spoke. Buxton said, "But one thing I couldn't endure to think of. It like to drove me wild. How'd I come to be caught? A man I'd knowed—not well, but we'd knowed each other since boy-hood—he turned me in for the reward. He betrayed me for money."

Jaysey met the sheriff's glance. He cleared his throat, "Jemmy—"

The ex-convict paid him no attention. He did not relax the grip of his fingers. The boy wiggled a bit, but didn't protest. Buxton went on, "Ever time they whupped me —and they whupped me aplenty—not like this boy's daddy will whup him—but with a big leather belt with brass studs in it—I thought of this man who'd put me where I was. Day and night I thought of it. You talk about gettin' somebody, you don't know what it is to hope for revenge, for years on end. I tried to break away. They caught me. More time to serve. More punishment.

"My thought of hurting this man that'd hurt me, it was like a burden I carried day and night. It give me no rest. It was a pain to me, a deep pain and a heavy burden. Then one day I couldn't stand it no more. I laid my burden down. Some of the other prisoners, they laughed at me for gettin' religion. No matter. Though I was still in jail, I felt free. I forgave this man. And as soon as I did, I was free of my pain."

Suddenly, he seemed to recall where he was. He smiled, relaxed his grip. The boy sighed. The color came into his face. Slowly he smiled back. Buxton turned around. "Why hello, Preacher—Sheriff—Mr. Jaysey—"

The sheriff said, "Time we got these kids back to town. Their folks'll be burning up the wires."

William said, "Jemmy—"

"Yes, Mr. Jaysey?"

"This man—the one who turned you in—"

But someone else finished the sentence for him. The boy rubbed one shoulder with his hand and asked, "What was his name?"

Buxton's battered face grew puzzled. Then his smile returned. "I don't know," he said. His voice seemed happy. "I can't remember." He looked at them all. "And it don't matter, anyway," he said "I laid my burden down. And I don't want to pick it up again." He nodded to them and went out into the night. "Board!" they heard him calling. "All aboard!"

The sheriff said, "Let's go." His eyes avoided Jaysey's. The two boys got up to leave. "Maybe you and Miz Lizzy'd like to ride back in the bus with your girls," Sheriff Wheeler said. "Don't think there's room in the car, now."

They all moved to the door, filed out of it.

One boy said to the other, "Forget what I said. I didn't really mean it."

William was the last to leave. His shoulders were bowed. He seemed very tired. He walked slowly, like a man with a heavy burden.

I Had a Hunch, And . . .
Talmage Powell

AFTER A STRANGELY TIMELESS INTERVAL, Janet realized she was dead.

She experienced only a little shock, and no fear. Perhaps this was because of the carefree way she had conducted her past life.

She had never felt so free. A thought wave her propulsion, she zipped about the great house, then outside, toward the great, clean open sky. Above, the stars were ever so bright and beautiful. Below, the lights of the suburban estate where she had been born and reared shone as if to answer the stars.

Janet was delighted with the whole experience. It confirmed some of the beliefs she had held, and it is always nice for one to have one's beliefs confirmed. It also excited the vivacious curiosity which had always been one of her major traits. And now there were ever so many more things about which to be curious.

She returned to the foyer of the house and looked at her lifeless physical self lying at the base of the wide sweeping stairway.

Whillikers, I was a very good-looking hunk of female, she decided. *Really I was.*

The body at the foot of the stairway was slender, clad in a simple black dinner dress. The wavy mass of black hair had spilled to rest fanwise on the carpet. The soft lovely face was calm—as in innocent, dreamless sleep.

Only the awkward twist and weird angle of the slim neck revealed the true nature of the sleep.

A quick ache smote Janet. *I must accept things. This—this is really so wonderful, but I do wish I—she—could have had just a little more time. . . .*

The great house was silent. Lights blazing on death, on stillness.

Janet remembered. She had returned unexpectedly to change shoes. Getting out of the car at the country club, she had snagged the heel of her left shoe and loosened it.

"I'll only be a little while," she had promised Cricket and Tom and Blake.

"We'll wait dinner," Blake had said, after she'd waved aside his insistence that he drive her home.

At home again, she had reached the head of the stairs when she heard someone in her bedroom.

She'd always possessed a cool nerve. She'd eased down the hallway. He'd been in there. Murgy. Dear old Murgy. Life hadn't begun without the memory of Murgy. He was ageless. He had worked for the family forever. Murgatroyd had been as much a part of Janet's life as the house, the giant oaks on the lawn, the car in the garage, over which Murgy lived in his little apartment.

She simply hadn't understood at first. Crouched in the hallway and peering through the crack of the partially opened door, she had seen a brand-new Murgy. This one had a chill face, but eyes that burned with determination. This one moved with much more deftness and decisiveness than the Murgy she'd always known.

He was stealing her jewelry. He was taking it from the small wall safe and replacing paste replicas. They were excellent replicas. They must have cost Murgy a great deal of money. But whatever the cost, it was pennies compared to the fortune he was slipping under his jacket.

She saw him compare a fake diamond bracelet with the real thing. The fakes were so good, she might have gone for years without knowing a large portion of her inheritance had been replaced by them.

As she saw the genuine diamond bracelet disappear into his pocket, she had gasped his name.

He had responded like a man jerking from a jolt of electricity. Frightened, she had turned, run. He had caught her at the head of the stairs.

She had tried to tell him how much his years of service meant, that she would have given him a chance to explain, a chance to straighten the thing out.

But he had given *her* no chance. He had pushed savagely at her with both arms. She had fallen, crying out, trying to grab something to break the fall.

She had struck hard. There had been one blinding flash, mingled with pain.

Murgy had followed her down. He had stood looking at her, wiping his hands on a handkerchief. He had listened, and heard no sound. She had come alone. Everything was all right. Even the heel on her left shoe had come off during her fall.

Murgy's decision was plain in his face. He would go to his quarters. Let her be discovered. Let her death be considered an accident.

Janet broke away from the study of what had once been her body.

Murgy, you really shouldn't have done it. There is a balance in the order of things and you have upset it. There is only one way you can restore the balance, Murgy. You must pay for what you have done. Besides, my freedom won't be complete until you do.

Janet was aware of a presence in the foyer.

Cricket had entered. Cricket and Tom and Blake, wondering why she hadn't returned, beginning to worry, deciding to see what was keeping her.

A willowy blonde girl, not too intelligent, but kind and eager to please, Cricket saw the body at the base of the stairway. She put her fists to her temples and opened her mouth wide.

Janet rushed to her side. In her world of silence, she couldn't hear Cricket screaming, but she knew that was what she was doing. Cricket's merry blue eyes were not merry now. They strained against their sockets with a terrible intensity.

Poor Cricket. I'm not in pain, Cricket.

She tried to touch Cricket with the touch of compassion. Cricket wasn't aware of this effort, Janet knew instantly. She wasn't here, as far as Cricket was concerned. She would never again be here for Cricket, or for any of the others.

Blake and Tom were beside Cricket now. Tom was

helping her to a deep couch. Blake was taking slow, halting steps toward the body at the foot of the stairs.

Blake kneeled beside the young, dead body. He reached as if he would touch it. Then his hands fell to his sides. He rose, his dark, handsome face pained.

He turned, stumbled to Tom and Cricket. Cricket had subsided into broken sobs. Tom sat with his arms about her shoulders. Shock and fright made the freckles on Tom's lean, pale face stand out sharply.

They were discussing the discovery. Janet could feel their horror, their sorrow. She could sense it, almost touch it. It was as if she could almost reach the edges of their essence, of their being, with her own essence and being.

Blake was picking up the telephone now. This would be for the doctor.

Before the doctor arrived, Murgy came in. Janet strained toward him. Then she recoiled, as from a thing dark and slimy.

He was speaking. *Saying he had heard a scream, no doubt.*

Then Blake stepped from in front of Murgy. And Murgy looked toward the stairs.

Cosmic pulsations passed through Janet as she slipped along with Murgy to the body at the stairway.

She could feel the fine control deep within him, the crouching of the dark, slimy thing as, in its wanton determination to survive, it braced the flesh and ordered the brain and arranged the emotions.

The emotions were in such a storm that Janet drew back. Murgy went to his knees beside the body and wept openly. *There was Blake now, helping Murgy to a chair. Everything was so dreadfully out of balance.*

She tried to get through to Blake. She strained with the effort. She succeeded only in causing Blake to look at Murgy a little strangely, as if something in Murgy's grief struck a small discord in Blake.

Blake went to fetch Murgy a glass of water. Janet turned her attention to Cricket and Tom. Tom's mind was resilient and strong. She battered at the edges of it, but it was too full of other things. Memories. Janet could vaguely

sense them. Memories that somehow concerned her and the
good times their young crowd had had.

Cricket was simply blank. Shocked beyond thinking.

Janet perched over the front doorway and beheld the
scene in its entirety.

*Look, people. He did it. Murgy's a murderer. He mustn't
be allowed to get away with it.*

Doctor Roberts came into the house. He spoke briefly
with the living and turned toward the dead. He stood
motionless for a moment. His grief spread like a black aura
all about him. It spread until it had covered the whole
room. He had delivered Janet, prescribed for her sniffles, set
the arm she'd broken trying to jump a skittish horse during
a summer vacation from college. He had sat by her all night
the night he'd broken the news to her that her parents had
been killed in a plane crash, that now she would have to
live in the great house with Murgy and a housekeeper to
look after her wants.

She flew to Doctor Roberts, remembering the way the
big, square face and white goatee had always symbolized
strength and intelligence to her.

*You must understand, Doctor. It was Murgy. He was
ever so lucky; everything worked devilishly for him, my
arrival alone, the broken shoe heel.*

Then she fell back, appalled. It was as if she had
bruisingly struck a solid black wall, the walls of a crypt
where Doctor Roberts had shut away a part of himself.
*She would never reach him, because he didn't believe. When
a man died, he died as a dog or a monkey died. That's
what Doctor Roberts maintained.*

Janet moved to a table holding an assortment of potted
plants. She studied the activities before her.

She saw Doctor Roberts complete his examination. He
talked with Blake. He looked at the broken shoe heel and
nodded.

He put a professional eye on Cricket. He reopened his
bag, took out a needle, and gave her a shot. Then he spoke
with Tom, and Tom took Cricket out.

The doctor was explaining something to Blake. At last,
Blake nodded his consent.

Janet felt herself perk up.

Of course, they'll phone the police. It's a routine, have-to measure when something like this happens.

She felt the dark, slimy thing in Murgy gather and strengthen itself, felt its evil smugness and confidence.

This was her last chance, Janet knew. The balance simply to be restored. Otherwise, she was liable to be earthbound until Murgy, finally, died and a higher justice thus restored the cosmic balance.

But what if they send someone like Doctor Roberts?

The policeman came at last.

He was a big man, had sandy hair and gray eyes and a jaw that looked as if it had been hacked from seasoned oak. His nose had been broken sometime in the past and reposed flagrantly misshapen on his face.

Janet hovered over him.

Look at Murgy!

For Pete's sake, one second there, when you walked in, it was naked in Murgy's eyes!

Intent on his job, the policeman walked to the stilled form at the foot of the stairway. He looked at the left shoe, then up the stairs.

After a moment, he walked up the stairs, examined the carpet, the railing. He measured the length of the stairs with his eyes.

Then he came slowly down the stairs.

He paused and looked at the beautiful girlish body.

His compassion came flooding out into the room. Janet felt as if she could ride the edges of it like a buoy.

It was a quiet, unguarded moment for him. Janet threw her will into the effort.

It was Murgy. Look at Murgy, the murderer!

He glanced at Murgy. But then, he glanced at the others too.

He began talking with Doctor Roberts.

Janet stayed close to the policeman.

If she could have met him in life, she knew they would have enjoyed a silent understanding.

I met a lot of people like that. Everybody meets people whom they like or distrust just by a meeting of the eyes.

You're feeling them out, forming opinions right now, by looking into their eyes, talking with them, letting the edges of your senses reach out and explore the edges of theirs.

I feel your respect for the doctor.

I feel you recoil now as you talk with Murgy. The dark, slimy thing is deep down, well hidden, but somehow you sense it.

But for Pete's sake, feeling it isn't enough. You must pass beyond feeling to realization.

Murgy killed me.

The balance simply has to be restored.

The policeman broke off his talk with Murgy. More official people had arrived. They took photographs. Two of them in white finally carried the body away on a stretcher.

Except for the policeman, the official people went away.

Blake went out. The doctor departed. Murgy was standing with tears in his eyes. The policeman touched Murgy's shoulder, spoke.

Janet was in the doorway, barring it. But Murgy didn't know she was there. He went across the lawn, to his apartment over the garage.

Only the policeman was left. He stood with his hat in his hands, looking at a spot at the base of the stairs with eyes heavy with sadness.

He was really younger than the rough face and broken nose made him appear.

Young and sad because he had seen beauty dead. Young and sad, and sensitive.

Janet pressed close to him. *It's all right, for me. You understand? There's no pain. It's beautiful here—except for the imbalance of Murgy's act.*

It wasn't an accident. You mustn't believe that. Murgy did it. You didn't like him. You sensed something about him.

Think of him! Think only of Murgy!

Don't leave yet. Ask yourself, are you giving up too easily. Shouldn't you look further?

He passed his hand through his hair. He seemed to be asking himself a question. He measured the stairway with his eyes.

She could sense the quiet, firm discipline that was in him, the result of training, of years of experience. The result of never ceasing to question, never stopping the mental probe for the unlikely, the one detail out of place.

Yes, yes! You feel something isn't quite right.

The shoe—if a girl came home to change it, would she go all the way upstairs and then start down again without changing it?

Oh, the question is clear and nettlesome in your mind.

It's a fine question.

Don't let it go. Follow it. Think about it.

He stood scratching his jaw. He walked all the way upstairs. Down the hallway. He looked in a couple of rooms, found hers.

In her room, he opened the closet. He looked at the shoes.

He stood troubled. Then he went back to the head of the stairs. Again he measured them with his eyes.

But finally, he shook his head and walked out of the house.

Come back! You must come back!

She couldn't reach him. She knew he wasn't coming back. So she perched on the roof of his speeding car as it turned a corner a block away.

He went downtown. He stopped the car in the parking lot at headquarters. He went into the building and entered his office.

Another man was there, an older man. The two talked together for a moment. The older man went out.

The policeman sat down at his desk. He picked up a pen and drew a printed form toward him.

Janet hovered over the desk.

You mustn't make out the form. You must not write it off as an accident.

Murgy did it.

He started writing.

It was murder.

He wrote a few lines and stopped.

Go get Murgy. He was the only one on the estate when it happened. Can't you see it had to be Murgy?

He nibbled at the end of the pen.

Think of the shoe. I went up, but I didn't change shoes.
He ran his finger down his crooked nose. He started writing again.

Okay, bub, if that's the way you want it, go ahead and finish the report. Call it an accident. But I'm not giving up. I'm sticking with you. I'll throw Murgy's name at you so many times you'll think you're suffering combat fatigue from being a cop too long.

Ready? Here we go, endlessly, my friend, endlessly. Murgy, Murgy, Murgy Murgymurgymurgy . . .

He drove home. He showered. He got in bed. He turned the light off.

After a time, he rolled over and punched the pillow. After another interval, he threw back the covers with an angry gesture, turned on the light, sat on the edge of the bed, and smoked a cigarette.

There was a telephone beside the bed and on the phone stand a pad of paper.

While he smoked, he doodled. He drew a spiked heel. He drew the outlines of a house. He wasn't a very good artist. He looked at the drawing of the house and under it he wrote: "No sign of forced entry. Only that servant around . . ."

He drew a pair of owlish eyes, and ringed them in black. He added some sharp lines for a face.

Then he ripped off the sheet of paper, wadded it and threw it toward the wastebasket. He snubbed out his cigarette, turned off the light for a second time, punched his pillow with a gesture betokening finality, and threw his head against it.

He reached the curtain of sleep. He started through it. Cells relaxing, the barriers began to waver, weaken.

She pressed in close.

MurgymurgymurgyMURGY!

He tossed and pulled the covers snug about his shoulders. Then he threw them off, got out of bed, and snapped on the light.

He was still agitated as he dressed and went out.

He sat in the dark car for many long minutes before

starting it. He drove aimlessly for a couple of blocks, his mind a pair of millstones grating against themselves. He stopped before a bar and went in.

He sat down at the end of the bar, alone. He had one, two, three drinks. His face was still troubled by nagging questions.

Two more drinks. They didn't help. The creases deepened in his cheeks.

Janet balanced atop a cognac bottle. *Better give Murgy a little more thought. Why not follow him, shadow him? He isn't resting easy. He'll want to get rid of those jewels in a shady deal now and be ready to run if the fakes are spotted.*

The policeman raised his gaze and looked at the television set over the bar. He stopped thinking about the long stairway, the broken heel, Murgy, and various possibilities. His mind snapped to what he was seeing on the TV set.

A local newscaster with doleful face was talking about her, her death. He was only a two dimensional image and she could sense nothing about him from this point. He was taking considerable time, and she could only guess that he was talking about her background, her family. There were some old newspaper pictures, one taken when she'd been helping raise money for the crippled children's hospital. She hadn't wanted any publicity for that, and she wished the newscast were less thorough.

There was a sudden disturbance down the bar. A fat man with a bald head and drink-flushed face was giving the TV set the Bronx cheer.

Janet felt quick displeasure. *Really, I was never the rich, degenerated hussy you're making me out, mister.*

The force of the mental explosion back down the bar caused Janet to rise to the ceiling. She saw that the fat man's exhibition had also disturbed her young policeman. He slammed out of the bar. And he was so mad he started across the street without looking.

Janet became a silent scream.

He looked up just in time to see the taxi hurtle around the corner. He tried to get out of the way. He'd had a drink too many.

Instantaneously, he became an empty shell of flesh and

blood, shortly destined to become dust, lying broken in
the middle of the street. A terrified but innocent cabbie was
emerging from his taxi, and a small crowd was pouring
out of the bar to join him.

This was defeat, Janet knew. Never had a defeat of the
flesh been so agonizing. The stars could have been hers.
Now the stars would have to wait, for a long, long time.
For as long as Murgy lived. It wasn't the waiting that
would be so hard. It was this entrapment in incompleteness,
this torture, this unspeakable pain of being inescapably en-
meshed in cosmic injustice.

She took her misery to the darkest shadow she could find
and lurked there awhile, until the scene in the street had
run its course, from arrival to departure of the police.

A bitter thought wave her propulsion, she returned to the
estate. She filtered through the roof and hovered in the
foyer.

While there had been hope, the foyer's full capacity for
torture had not reached her. Now she felt it.

"Hello, Beautiful."

Where had the thought come from? She swirled like a
miniature nebula.

"Take it easy I'm right here."

He swirled beside her. *Her policeman.*

"You!"

"Sure. I was so amazed at where I found myself I didn't
get to you while you were hiding near the accident. You
know, you *feel* even more beautiful than you looked."

"Why, thanks for the compliment. And your own home-
liness, fellow, was all of the flesh. But don't you concern
yourself with me."

"Why not?"

"I'm stuck here. You didn't catch Murgy."

"I had a hunch about that guy . . ."

"Hunch? Hah! It was me trying to get the guilt of the
old boy across to you."

"Really? Well, I was going to keep an eye on him."

"I was after you to do that, too. See, I caught him stealing my jewels."

"I had to go and ruin everything!"

"But you didn't mean to barge in front of that cab."

"Just the same, I'll spend eternity being sorry. Sure you can't come with me?"

"Nope. Just go quickly."

He was gone. She felt his unwilling departure. It was the final straw of torture.

"Look, honey, my name's Joe."

He was back.

"I got this idea. It's worth a try at least."

It was so good having him back.

"My superior officer, Lieutenant Hal Dineen. He's the sharpest, most tenacious cop ever to carry a badge. That report of mine, to start with, is going to raise a question in his mind. The same facts you were trying to get over to me are there for him to find. I just bounced over to headquarters and back. Just a look told me my fray with that taxi has knocked his mental guards to smithereens. He was at his desk, reading that last report of mine. If you alone could do what you did, consider what the two of us trying real hard can do if we hit Dineen, in his present state, with full thought force."

Janet bounced to the rooftop. Joe was beside her.

"Janet, Dineen is razor-sharp at playing hunches. He believes in them. All set to hit him with the grandfather of all hunches, the results of which he'll talk about for a lifetime?"

"Let's." *Let's, darling.*

Lieutenant Hal Dineen was talking to a fellow officer, "I dunno. Just one of those things. Comes from being a cop, I guess, from having the old subconscious recognize and classify information the eyes, ears, and hands miss. Just a hunch I had about this old family retainer. We all get 'em—these hunches. Me, especially, I'm a great one for 'em. And this one I couldn't shake and so I figured . . ."

A Killing in the Market
Robert Bloch

I MAY NOT have much time to set this down.

To make things worse, the pen leaks, and there isn't very much paper. You'd think that for forty dollars a day, the hotel would furnish a decent pen. At least they could replace the supply of stationery once in awhile. Of course, I suppose I could call room service and ask for more, but I don't dare to have anyone nosing around.

It's just that I want to write this out while I still have the chance. Maybe it will help explain a few things. At least it might be of interest to a few eager beavers—the kind of people who've always dreamed of a chance to make a big killing in the stock market.

That was my idea. I wanted to make a killing. And now I have, only—

I suppose I ought to begin at the beginning. And say that my name is Albert Kessler, and up until a little over three months ago I worked in Wall Street. I was a clerk in a brokerage house. Maybe I'd better not mention the name of the firm. It isn't important, anyway.

Up until then, nothing was important. Including myself. I was just another guy, holding down just another job. My idea of a big deal was to get out fifteen minutes early and catch a seat in the subway, instead of having to stand up all the way home. That's another laugh—home. One furnished room, in the Bronx. A small order of nothing. But that's all I had. That, and the big dream.

I guess everybody who ever worked in the Street has had the same dream. It's one of those things you think about when you bounce around in the subway, or on the mattress in your crummy room. You can't help but think about it, and hope that tomorrow it's going to come true.

Tomorrow, that's always when you're going to get the

break—when you'll just happen to run into this character with the golden touch. He's a plunger, and every time he plunges he comes up smelling like a rose. Somehow you manage to make friends with him, and pretty soon he's giving you the word on a good thing, and before you know it you're a character yourself. A real big operator.

Sure, I know what it sounds like. But after you spend a little time working in the Street, you can't help but think that way. Because you occasionally see the dream come true. Bernard Baruch isn't the only one who ever made a killing. You hear stories about guys who started out as runners and ended up buying their own seats on the Exchange. Sometimes they made all their money on the Big Board, and sometimes they branched off into investing in their own firms. The oil men, those Greek shipping magnates, people like that; they prove it happens.

But it doesn't happen to everyone; not to guys who just moon around and wish. You've got to do more than dream. You've got to keep your eyes open and figure the angles. And you've got to wait.

That's what I did. For over two years I waited. And I planned. I saved my dough, too. Not much—a pitiful three thousand. But at least I held onto it. A lot of the other dreamers aren't willing to save and wait. They're suckers for every crazy rumor on the Street, and they use the Dow-Jones like a scratch-sheet. It's five bucks on Steel to win, or ten bucks on Industrials to place or Utilities to show. The *Journal* is their racing form, and they make graphs and charts and follow stock performance records back for years. They play systems or they play hunches—but all of them go for broke.

That two-dollar window stuff wasn't for me. I didn't believe in tips or theories. Sure, the Market is a gamble, but gamblers aren't always winners. The winner, in the long run, is the man who has a sure thing from the start.

I kept my eyes open trying to spot that winner. Instead of studying the Market, I studied the customers.

And that's how I found Lon Mariner.

There's no sense going into all the details of how I made up my mind. Half a dozen times beforehand, I thought I'd located my man—a big investor, who consistently moved in at the right time, then moved out again after a quick profit. But each time, sooner or later, the customer I had my eye on pulled a goof, or started hedging with gilt-edge stuff at a small profit. Over the years I kept track of several investors; in New York, or in our branch offices.

But it wasn't until three months ago that I made my discovery. Lon Mariner, who always pulled a sure thing out of the hat. He put fifteen thousand into a small aircraft company three days before they landed a big Navy contract. He pulled out with fifty thousand and bought into some electronics outfit I never heard of—until they declared a split, then a dividend, and bounced up eighteen points. He took his profits and went into oil, dumping his stock the morning before a nose-dive. Next there was a flier in a Texas railroad that was gobbled up by a bigger combine within a week. By this time I was really following his orders, which came in through our Frisco office. And I was surprised to find that after a month or so he was operating out of Cleveland. But the pattern continued. What he bought didn't make sense; the important thing was that everything he touched turned to gold. Copper, radar, TV in Cleveland; then a big utilities deal out of Boston. He never missed on timing. In eleven weeks he was in on every spectacular rise, every major split across the Board. I figured he'd run his fifteen thousand up to several million. Then he placed his next whopping order out of our Chicago office.

That's when I quit my job and went to Chicago.

All I had was three thousand dollars and this wild idea of mine. At least I thought it was a wild idea, after I actually got on the plane. Here I was, chasing halfway across the country to locate a perfect stranger—or maybe a stranger who wasn't so perfect—in hopes that I'd get him to cut me in on his big deal.

I did some sweating on that flight when I really took stock of the situation. After all, what did I know about this Lon Mariner, anyway? He wasn't in *Who's Who*. And he didn't have a D&B rating, either. I hadn't dared to make any direct inquiries through any of our branch offices. All I really knew about him was that he was the guy I was looking for—the guy with the golden touch. From now on, I'd have to play it by ear.

The minute I got off the airport limousine at the Palmer House, I took a cab over to our Chicago office on LaSalle Street. I still had my company ID card—so I forgot to turn it in, is that a crime?—and I flashed it. I said I'd been sent out here to contact one of our clients, and had Mr. Mariner been in today?

Well, it turned out Mr. Mariner hadn't been in—today or any day. His orders came by phone and his bank drafts by mail. I went clear up to the Vice-President in Charge Of, but nobody could tell me anything more about the man.

But I did find out he was staying at a hotel on the Gold Coast. *This* hotel.

I hotfooted it over yesterday afternoon, and plunked down my forty bucks for this room—complete with air conditioning, television, and a lousy pen.

Forty bucks was only the start of my investment. Ten bucks more made sure that the Room Clerk put me on the same floor—he even showed me Mariner's name on the register, and his suite number. It was 701, right down the corridor from my room. He didn't remember much about Mariner's appearance, because he hadn't seen him since. Said he'd come in alone, without very much luggage, and that he was "average-looking." Medium height, brown hair, middle-aged.

I spent another ten bucks on the bellboy. All he could tell me was that Mariner ordered all his meals sent up to him, and that he didn't go out much except in the mornings when the maid-service cleaned up.

By this time it was almost seven o'clock, and the maids were off duty. I had to settle for a talk with the waiter who served him his meals, a guy named Joe Franscetti.

For the usual ten, Franscetti said yes, he'd just come down from Mr. Mariner's room after clearing away the supper dishes. Apparently, Mariner hadn't made any impression on him at all; I got the same vague description of an "average-looking" guy. The waiter couldn't remember anything he'd ever said to him, or even how he usually dressed.

"But I can tell you what he had for dinner," he said. "Shrimp cocktail, the prime ribs—medium rare, I think it was—baked potato, Waldorf salad, coffee, apple pie. And you know what he tipped? A lousy half a buck!"

I thanked him and went away. It was a little discouraging. I hadn't come all this way to find out that Lon Mariner liked his meat medium rare. And even the fact that a guy on a five-million-dollar winning streak is a poor tipper didn't mean very much to me.

There didn't seem to be anything I could do at the moment. No sense going to the house dick. It had been risky enough asking the questions I'd asked, because the last thing I wanted was to call attention to myself. I suppose everyone figured I was a private eye, and that was bad enough, but at least it was some kind of an excuse.

Anyway, I'd learned nothing useful, and from now on I was on my own. So about seven-thirty I ended up back in my room, with the door open. If I sat in a chair at a certain angle I could keep my eye on 701. Just in case Mariner *did* go out.

Of course, there was nothing to prevent me from just marching down the hall and knocking on his door. Except that I wasn't ready for that yet. Before talking to Mariner, I had to make up my mind about him. When I did speak to him, my conversation was going to be mighty important. I couldn't afford to muff the deal, and I had to decide what I intended to say. And that would depend on sizing up my man, first.

There was just one thing running through my mind right now. Mariner must be some kind of a nut.

On the face of it, there wasn't anything particularly screwy about what I'd heard concerning him; lots of quiet, middle-aged guys are a little on the timid side, and prefer to keep to themselves if they live alone. But under the circumstances, the pattern didn't make sense. If *I'd* cleaned up millions in the market in three months, *I* wouldn't be hiding out by myself in a hotel room, and that's for darn sure.

So he was probably a psycho, like all those eccentric

recluses you hear about who end up dying in a basement with a fortune in cash stuck under the mattress.

I sat there for a long time, thinking about it. And the more I thought, the worse I felt. Because it's pretty hard to get close to that kind of a nut. They're the suspicious type, delusions of persecution and everything. They don't trust strangers, and nobody's their friend.

On the other hand, there was something wrong with the picture. I was paying forty bucks a day. And Mariner, even if he was a stingy tipper, must be shelling out close to a hundred for his suite. Besides, during the last few months, he'd moved from Frisco to Cleveland to Boston to Chicago —and trips like that cost dough. Even if he was making millions, he wouldn't be inclined to spend an extra dime if he was just another eccentric. Those guys hole up in the slums and stay put, and they eat stale crackers instead of shrimp cocktails.

So there must be some other reason why Mariner was keeping himself under wraps. I got a sudden hunch.

Could it be that he was the stooge or front-man for some syndicate?

That made a little better sense to me. Sure, it could explain a lot of things. Including why he stuck to his room. Probably he got his information or his orders by phone. It was a cinch one or the other came from someplace, unless he just got tips on the market out of dreams.

I was beginning to get a terrible yen to visit his room and see if I could spy on him while he was under the influence of H, or operating his ouija board, or whatever he did. Maybe he kept a collection of shrunken heads, and they talked to him.

On the other hand, it might be a lot smarter to check the switchboard girl tomorrow and see if she'd just keep track of any phone calls coming in or going out of his suite, and slip me the word.

I looked at my watch. Almost ten o'clock, and nothing had happened. I was tired. Better turn in and sleep on it. In the morning I'd decide what to do.

So I got up and went over to the door to close it.

Just as *his* door opened, and he came out.

I knew it was Mariner the minute I saw him. Middle-aged, middle-sized, brown-haired; he wore a plain blue suit and a white shirt, and the face above the collar was the kind you could forget even while you were looking at it.

I guess I've seen ten thousand such faces in my time—crowded into elevators, jammed into subways, bobbing along the street. Looking at them had never made me sweat, but I was sweating now. Because this face was worth five million bucks. Lon Mariner, the man with the golden touch.

Now I got a look at his back. He was trying his door, making sure it was locked. Maybe he kept a lot of cash inside. Maybe I could stick around and pick the lock. No, that was too dangerous. What I had to do was follow him and pick his brains.

I put on my coat while he walked over to the elevator. I figured I could dash out and make it just in time, but I figured wrong. Because the car stopped before I reached my door, and he got in.

Then I was swearing, and running down the stairs. I hit the lobby in one minute flat, but he wasn't there and the elevator was already going up again. I could see the lights flickering on the numerals—two, then three, then four.

I shook my head. Should I wait for the car to come down again and talk to the elevator boy, hoping he'd remember which way the man in the blue suit had gone? Or should I dash outside and try to find him?

I decided to get going. I started across the lobby, trying not to break into a run, and scooted past the entrance to the cocktail lounge. Something caught my eye as I went by. The back of a blue suit.

I stopped.

Mariner was sitting at the bar, all alone, way down at the end.

The sweat rolled down my sides as I walked into the place. I chose a stool about twenty feet away from him; there wasn't anybody between us. In fact, outside of a couple off over in a booth, we had the whole joint to ourselves.

The bartender, a fat guy with a mustache, was pouring

Mariner a drink. Cognac, from the looks of the glass. He saw me and came down to my end of the bar.

I ordered a beer and swivelled around on the stool so that I could get a good look at my man.

The waiter had certainly been right; Lon Mariner was "average-looking." I didn't get a clue from his ready-made clothes, and there wasn't a hint of anything unusual in his ready-made face, either. He was just another guy.

The more I studied him, the worse I felt. I'd been sure that after I had a chance to get a close look at him, I could size him up and figure out the best way to approach him. But he just sat there, a bump in a blue suit on an overstuffed log. He didn't seem to be enjoying his drink, he wasn't listening to the radio, and he never looked around at the bartender or at me. He had about as much life as a window dummy, and he wasn't nearly as handsome.

All at once he signaled for another drink. And when the bartender brought the bottle and poured, he slugged down the shot and told him to refill. Then, after he paid, he mumbled something and the bartender left the bottle standing there on the bar.

That told me something, at last. That, and the way he sat there, all stiff and frozen.

He was frozen, all right, because he was afraid. I recognized the symptoms, now. He was scared to death about something and even more scared that he'd show it. So he sat and drank.

I had my cue, now. I waited until he'd poured and downed his fourth drink. Then I glanced around, checking to see that the place was still almost empty, and slid off my stool. I walked down along the bar and stood next to him. He could see me in the bar mirror, and I noticed the way his fingers tightened around his empty glass.

"Mr. Mariner," I said. "I've been looking for you."

If he'd turned around and thrown the glass at me, that would have been one thing. If he'd turned pale, gasped, or slumped to the floor in a dead faint, that would have been another. But what he *didn't* do was still more effective.

He didn't move.

He'd been frozen before; now he was dead. He tightened

up, all over, as if *rigor mortis* was setting in. I had the feeling he'd stopped breathing, just stopped completely.

"I want to talk to you, Mr. Mariner," I murmured.

He didn't turn his head and his lips never moved. But a sound came out of him, and then faint words.

"You must be mistaken. My name's not Mariner."

I shrugged. "Of course it isn't. But that's the name you signed on the hotel register. That's the name you've been using on all your business deals. I know."

He reached out and spilled himself another drink. Not poured—spilled. I watched him do it, waited while he wavered the glass up to his lips and gulped. Then he whispered again.

"How did you find me?"

"That isn't important," I answered. "I've been keeping an eye on you for quite awhile."

"Then I was wrong all along, wasn't I? I thought I could get away with it. But they knew all the time, didn't they?"

"I'm all alone, Mr. Mariner."

"Yes. But they sent you."

I hesitated, then decided how to play it. "Nobody sent me. This was my own idea. I've been studying your stock market operations for months. You see, I work for the firm you've been doing business with. And I wanted to talk to you about your methods."

"My—methods?"

For the first time there was a recognizable expression on his face. You could almost call it a smile. He turned his head just a trifle and stared at me. "Then I was wrong. You're just an—an ordinary citizen?"

"Very ordinary, I assure you. But I have an extraordinary curiosity about you. Or about any man who can do what you've been doing in the investment field. I thought we might discuss your methods."

He was really smiling, now. He poured another drink, and his hand was perfectly steady.

"Well, I don't know—"

He was confident once more, ready to brush me off. I knew how to handle that.

"Listen, Mr. Mariner. I'm not the nosey type, but you've

already told me enough so that I know you're in some kind of trouble. You don't exactly welcome publicity, do you? I mean, you wouldn't want any stories in the papers about mysterious millionaires, or men traveling under assumed names who have secret methods of beating the stock market. I could go to the phone right now and call the reporters—"

"You wouldn't!"

"Of course I wouldn't. Because you're going to talk to me, instead. Just me. And if you can tell me what I think you can, I'll have every reason to keep my own mouth shut in the future, just the way you do. There it is, Mr. Mariner—my cards are on the table. I want in."

"All right. We'll talk."

"Good."

"But not here. Not like this. In my room."

"Fine. Let's go up." I waited for a moment, then repeated it louder. "Let's go up."

But he wasn't listening to me.

He wasn't looking at me, either. He was staring into the bar mirror. I followed his glance.

Behind us, in the doorway of the cocktail lounge, stood a tall blonde. She had, among other things, the biggest pair of eyes I'd ever seen. She was worth looking at for a number of reasons, but her eyes were what held me.

The eyes held Mariner, too. He looked at her and his mouth opened and closed, and he froze up again. Really froze.

She didn't smile, and she didn't say anything, and she didn't even come closer. She just gave him that long look and then she beckoned.

Mariner stood up. "Excuse me," he muttered. "I must go now. I have an engagement."

"What about our talk?" I said.

"Oh, yes. Suppose we say ten o'clock tomorrow morning, in my room?"

I grabbed his arm. "You wouldn't try to pull a sneak, now would you? Remember what I said about the reporters."

"I remember."

"All right, see you at ten, then. But no funny business. I mean it, Mr. Mariner."

"I promise."

And then he was walking over to her, following her out of the place. I watched them go, saw them head across the lobby in the direction of the elevators. He couldn't find an exit that way, and I was pretty sure he wasn't looking for one—not with that tall blonde on his arm. In a way I didn't blame him for cancelling his appointment and putting me off until tomorrow. If a blonde like that ever beckoned to me, I'd cancel my appointments, too. I doubt if I'd be ready to see anyone even at ten the next morning.

But I'm still the suspicious type. I waited a few minutes, then got up and went out to the desk. The Room Clerk on duty was my ten buck boy.

I leaned across the counter and flipped a bill his way, very quietly.

He palmed it, just as quietly. "Yes, sir?"

"About Mr. Mariner," I said. "He didn't check out, did he?"

"No party by that name checked out, no sir."

"Well, in case he does, any time between now and to-morrow morning, I want you to call me. And right away, before he gets past the desk here."

"Certainly, but—"

"But what?"

The clerk was frowning. "I don't believe we *have* a party by that name here at the hotel."

I knew how to frown, too. "What do you mean, you don't have such a party? Lon Mariner, in Suite 701. You're the guy who tipped me off about him in the first place."

"I am? You must be mistaken, sir."

"Now, look—"

"You look, sir." The clerk flipped through the registration list. "Here's our guest-entries for the past week. No Mariner, is there? Are you sure you have the right name?"

"Am I sure? You showed me, yesterday. Give me that!" I grabbed and squinted. I saw my own name, and ran my eyes along the signatures above it. Paige, Stein, Tenn, Klass, Phillips, Graham—no Mariner.

"What kind of a business is this?" I was getting a funny feeling in my stomach. "Who's in Suite 701?"

"Let's look at the card-file. Over here, sir." He stepped to the next cage, where the billing entries were kept. He pulled out a yellow card. "Suite 701 has been vacant all week," he told me. "Just rented it tonight. Party named Fairborn. Here, see for yourself."

The funny feeling spread from my stomach upwards. My heart was pounding.

"But that's Mariner's suite," I said. "Little middle-aged guy, with a blue suit. You must have seen him going through the lobby just now, with a big blonde—"

The clerk shook his head. "No, sir, I didn't."

"But he was just in the bar; I talked to him."

"I'm sorry, sir—"

I turned my back and ran for the elevator. By the time I got to the seventh floor, my heart was in my mouth; and it wasn't from the fast ride, either.

I went down the corridor, right to 701, and banged on the door. My heart was in my mouth, but I could still talk. And when the door opened, I did.

"Mr. Mariner," I said. Then my voice trailed off. I was looking at the blonde with the big eyes. And she was looking at me.

"You have the wrong room, I believe."

"I don't. Where's Mariner?"

"Who?"

"The guy in the blue suit. You came up here with him less than half an hour ago. This is his room."

She shook her head. "Sorry, but you're mistaken. This is my room. I'm Miss Fairborn."

"But I saw you two together—"

The big eyes narrowed. "Now, wait a minute. I've been in this room ever since I arrived this evening. I don't know what you're talking about. If you doubt my word, you can check with the desk downstairs."

"I already did. But I know you and Mariner were together, I saw him leaving the bar with you."

"Ah. The bar. You were drinking there."

"Never mind that stuff. I'm not drunk! What'd you do

with Mariner?"

The door opened a trifle more. A man put his head out behind Miss Fairborn. He was a big man, with steel-gray hair, and he didn't look like Mariner at all. He looked like trouble.

"What goes on here?" he demanded.

Miss Fairborn shrugged. "I don't know. Some drunk looking for a friend. You'd better handle him, Harry."

"Glad to."

But I wasn't being handled. I backed away. "All right," I said. "So I made a mistake. I'm sorry."

Harry started to say something, and then stepped aside. I recognized the waiter, Joe Franscetti. He was coming out, wheeling a service table.

I waved at the three of them. "Excuse it please," I muttered. "I'll go quietly."

And I went, around the corner, hearing the door close behind me. I stood there, waiting until Joe Franscetti caught up with me. He wheeled his table along, head down. I stepped out and grabbed his elbow.

"What gives?" I asked. "Where's Mariner?"

"Who? What's that again, mister?"

"I asked where's Mariner? The guy in 701?"

"But I just come from there. You saw me. There's this dame and her boyfriend, they just had dinner."

"I know. Only that's Mr. Mariner's room. You served him all last week, you said so. Remember?"

"Mister, are you all right?"

"Of course I am. But everybody else has gone crazy. Now look here, you told me about Mariner yourself. The brown-haired guy in the blue suit, the one who only tipped fifty cents. Prime ribs rare, Waldorf salad."

"Mister, that room's been vacant all week. I never saw anyone like you say, and I never saw you before, either. You better lie down, you don't look so good."

I knew how I looked, but there was no sense wasting time. There was still the bell-captain; he'd know if a certain bellboy was on duty.

Downstairs I went. I found the bell-captain. My boy was on, tonight, and I caught him over in a corner of the lobby. This time I decided to make another investment.

"Here," I said, waving the bill under his nose. "This is a hundred bucks, see it?"

"Yes, sir."

"Now I've no idea what they might have paid you to clam up, but I've got a hunch they didn't go higher than twenty. So you might as well sell out to the highest bidder."

"I don't follow you, sir."

"It's very simple. Yesterday you and I had a little talk together. I was asking you questions about a man named Lon Mariner. In Suite 701. You described him to me, said he never went out except while the maids were cleaning up. Right?"

His eyes watched the hundred-dollar bill as it waved under his nose. Then he shook his head.

"Sorry, sir. I don't remember anything like that. I mean, I couldn't have told you such a thing, because 701 was vacant until this evening. I know for a fact—I took the party up myself just a few hours ago. A big blonde."

The hundred went back into my pocket and I headed back into the bar. It was still deserted, and the fat bartender came right over.

"Yes?"

"Remember me?" I asked. "I was in here earlier this evening."

"That's right."

Well, at least he admitted *I* had been here. Now I was ready to try for double or nothing.

"Remember the guy I was talking to?"

Silence.

"He left before I did, with a blonde."

"A big blonde?" The bartender brightened. "Sure, she was in here just a couple minutes ago. I served her a—I forget just what."

"She was in here before then, looking for this guy in the blue suit. He sat down at the end of the bar, drinking cognac. I spoke to him. Then she came along and they left together. Now do you recall him?"

The bartender shook his head. "I didn't see them. I didn't see you talking to anyone, either. You were all alone." He wiped the bar. "What's the matter, sir? You don't look so good."

"I don't feel so good," I told him. "Go away."

He went away and I sat there. No use talking any more. He wouldn't remember. None of them remembered. But I did.

I remembered an old English movie they keep reviving on television. *The Lady Vanishes*. This dame sees another dame and talks to her, and later everybody swears she doesn't exist. Of course she does; she's been kidnapped by spies.

Then there's the yarn that pops up every now and then about the woman in the hotel room; she disappears, too. I guess it started way back in the 1890s—it was supposed to have happened in Paris, during some kind of International Exposition. Turned out the woman had cholera and they hushed everything up in order to avoid a panic when she died. They even repapered her room overnight.

Come to think of it, I'd read a lot of detective novels with the same idea. And usually there was a dame involved, and a spy or murder plot.

Somehow I couldn't swallow it in connection with Mariner. Spies don't play the market. And I didn't think he had cholera, either, or even Asiatic flu.

But he *was* scared.

That I remembered. He'd been scared when I talked to him, wondering if *they* had sent me. So who were *they*? The Syndicate, maybe? He'd recognized the blonde, and gone along quietly. Gone along up to the suite, where the gray-haired man named Harry was waiting. He'd gone along, even though he was scared to death.

Scared to death. Was that it? Had they killed him?

It didn't seem logical, from any angle. You don't kill the goose that lays five million golden eggs. You can't get away with it, even in Chicago, in a swank hotel.

But they had gotten away with *something*. And that was the screwiest part of it. They'd made everybody forget Lon Mariner had even existed, including people who'd seen him just a little while before he vanished. They'd removed his name from the registry, and even from the billing cards.

Was it just bribery? I doubted it, somehow. You can't take such chances. Sooner or later somebody would come looking for Mariner and put on the pressure. Clerks, waiters, bellboys couldn't be trusted to keep their mouths shut when the heat was on. Somebody would come, and someone would sing. Bribery wasn't good enough.

How about threats? That might work. But the people I'd just talked to didn't seem frightened. They were just puzzled. It was as if they actually believed that Lon Mariner had never existed.

That was the point I kept coming back to.

Why was it so important to make sure nobody believed there had ever been such a man?

And *how* had they managed the trick? If the deal involved murder, then certainly the killers would be more interested in concealing their presence than the presence of the victim. Yet the blonde had registered openly, showed herself around. She'd even come back here to the bar, probably while I was out in the lobby, and talked to the bartender. He said she ordered a drink from him, he couldn't remember what.

He couldn't remember—

I got a flash. A flash of those enormous eyes, and the two of them in here, all alone. The blonde leaning over the bar and telling him he couldn't remember. Not bribing him, not threatening him, but *telling* him. Hypnotizing him into forgetting.

Wild?

Perhaps, but I was wild now, too. When plain facts don't make sense, you've got to look for something fancy. And hypnotism works. It works fast, under the right conditions, with the right operators. That blonde would be the right operator. She could get close to the clerk or the bellboy; they'd look—being men—and they'd listen. And the waiter, Joe Franscetti, had been right up there in the room with her, serving a meal. That left the bartender to deal with. So she slipped down here and slipped him a mental Mickey.

I felt a little better, but not much. Because Mariner was still missing, and I didn't know why. And *they* knew that *I* knew.

What I needed now was an ace in the hole. But I didn't have one. The best I could do was a gun in the suitcase. At the time, I'd worried a lot about packing one along. It seemed risky, and I really didn't expect to use threats on Mariner. Now I was glad I had it.

Because there was only one thing left for me to do. I'd have to go up to my room, get the gun, and knock on the door of Suite 701 again.

I got up and went out into the lobby. I took the elevator. I got off at the seventh floor. I tiptoed down the hall, past 701, to my own room. I took out the key and opened my door very quietly. I stepped in.

And then I stumbled, reaching for the light. I started to swear, under my breath, but I should have prayed instead. Because my having stumbled is what must have saved me.

The blow came out of the darkness behind the door, and if it had landed on my head, I'd have been a goner. As it was, my shoulder almost broke. But I ducked, and turned, and was just coming up with a right when two things happened simultaneously.

The light clicked on, and the man named Harry stuck a gun in my ribs.

"Now, march," he suggested.

We marched. There was nobody in the corridor to watch the parade go by. Nobody cheered when we halted before the door to 701.

He knocked. The door opened and Miss Fairborn looked out at Harry. "Did you get him?" she whispered.

"Yes," Harry murmured. "I got him." He pushed me into the room and closed the door.

"Then why didn't you knock him out?" she asked.

"Changed my mind," Harry said. "I think we might have other plans." He winked. "Understand?"

Miss Fairborn nodded, then turned. Those great big beautiful eyes stared at me.

"Cut it out," I said. "I don't hypnotize easy."

She sighed. "I know. That's why I didn't try. It wouldn't work on you because you wouldn't cooperate. You were too suspicious."

"Sorry. That's my nature."

"I'm sorry, too. If only you hadn't come, if only you'd go away now—but of course it's too late."

I looked across the room at the bed. "Where's the money?" I asked. "I thought it might be piled up here, ready for shipping."

Harry rubbed his chin with his free hand. I knew where the other one was, of course—it was holding the gun. And I knew where the gun was, too—still in my ribs.

"You had to guess, didn't you?" he said.

"Yes. I guessed. So where is it, might I ask?"

"You're in no position to ask anything, but I'll tell you. The money has already been shipped."

"And Mr. Mariner?"

"He's been shipped, too. Or will be, soon."

"Then it's like I thought. Murder."

"You did a lot of thinking, didn't you?"

"Why not?" I shrugged. "I knew Mariner was afraid for his life. That's why he kept running from city to city; that's why he holed up here. He practically turned blue when I spoke to him and he admitted *they* were after him. I didn't know what he was talking about until Miss Fairborn showed up. He was twice as frightened then, but he went along with her. So it all adds up, doesn't it? We were after the same thing—the secret of how he managed to make all that dough in such a hurry.

"The only difference is, I was working alone, and I intended to go about it in a nice way. You teamed up and put on the pressure. You were ready to threaten him, ready to kill him. And you did. I still can't understand how you figured you'd get away with it, but you did."

I paused as another thought struck me. "How did you manage to erase his name from our company records? Was it hypnosis again—the way you operated here in the hotel?"

Miss Fairborn nodded. "We have teams operating in every major city."

"That must cost dough. Of course, with five million involved—"

"Multiply it by ten," Harry said. "Mariner just made a little extra on the side, after he thought he'd sneaked away from us."

"From you?"

"You got your story a bit twisted. You see, we all work for the same outfit?"

"Syndicate?"

"Not the one you mean. It's a group of investment people. Their names don't matter. Let's just say they are wealthy and influential people who want to become still more wealthy and influential. They are in a position to get advance tips on a lot of inside deals—but there are laws governing the right to speculate independently in the affairs of your own company. So they conceived this idea of pooling their resources, setting up a private organization to make investments. As long as secrecy is maintained, they can make many millions in profits each year. All they needed was a front man."

"Mariner?"

"Exactly. A nobody from nowhere. Someone who followed orders; and a few trained people like us to keep an eye on him, check up to make sure he didn't get out of line. And it worked well, for the past few years. He must have brought in well over fifty million in stocks and bonds alone."

"But no one man could make that much money without making headlines as well. And I never heard of him until I stumbled across his trail three months ago, as a small investor."

"Exactly. Up until three months ago, his name wasn't Mariner. He used half a dozen other names over the years. That was part of the plan, to keep switching identities. And that was part of our job—to go around, when he changed his name, and erase memories of his previous existence. As I told you, we have similar operatives all over the country.

"Then, about three months ago, he decided to change his name on his own. He'd been armed with advance information, told what to invest and where to invest it. So he decided to skip out on us and work for himself. He took the Mariner name, started to dodge around the country. In ninety days he managed to pile up close to five million in cash profits. Then we caught up with him." Harry rubbed his chin again.

"Why are you telling me all this?" I asked.

He grinned. "Because I like your face."

"You're not going to try to kill me, too," I said. "You couldn't get away with that."

"Certainly not." He took the gun out of my ribs. "Here, you might as well have this, too." And he held the weapon out to me.

"But—"

"Go ahead, take it. It isn't loaded, anyway. Besides, it's your gun. I found it in your suitcase."

I blinked. "Why—"

Miss Fairborn smiled at me. "I think I know what Harry has in mind," she said. "He's asking you to join us. Aren't you, dear?"

"That's right," Harry said.

"You see," she said, "now we need someone to take Mr. Mariner's place. And since you seem to be alone in the world—"

"Exactly." Harry nodded pleasantly. "An ideal candidate."

"What if I don't like the idea?" I asked.

"Nonsense! That's why you followed Mr. Mariner, wasn't it?" Miss Fairborn said. "Because you wanted to make millions. That's been your big dream for a long time, hasn't it? Well, this is an opportunity to make your dream come true. From now on you'll be doing just that. You'll go from city to city—under a variety of names, of course—and you'll invest a fortune in securities. By the time the first year is ended you'll probably take in more cash than anyone else in the market today. What more could you ask from life?"

"But I won't be allowed to keep it. And I'll have to live under cover, in hotels, with people like you spying on me night and day, watching every move I make."

"The penalty of wealth," Miss Fairborn said.

"I won't have anything, not even a name. Nobody will know me, or even remember me after you've erased their memories."

"But think of the romance of being a man of mystery."

"I am thinking of it," I said. "And I don't like it. I don't like your proposition, and I don't like you. What's there to prevent me from just walking out of here, going to the police, and telling them your whole story? For that matter, I can probably get them to find Mariner's body."

"Probably," said Harry. "Suit yourself. But if you change your mind within the next hour, come on back. We'll be waiting right here for you."

"I won't be back," I told him, opening the door.

"Yes you will," Miss Fairborn called after me. "This is what you've always wanted. I'm sure you'll see it our way."

But, as I walked down the hall to my room, I didn't see it their way. I didn't understand it at all. They admitted murdering Mariner and they could have murdered me, too, just to be on the safe side. If their story was true, it would be worth the extra risk. Instead, they offered me this fantastic proposition—this living death. Why?

I didn't see it. Not until I was actually back in my room, not until I walked into the bathroom and saw him lying there in the tub, with a bullet in his forehead. The pillow through which it had been fired lay on the floor next to the tub. They'd thought of everything. The pillow had muffled the sound of the shot. And that's why Harry had come to my room. He'd murdered Mariner with *my* gun. No wonder he'd given it back to me!

Yes, I saw it now. The corpse was in my room, the fingerprints were on my gun. I'd been looking for Mariner, told everyone about him. Running away wouldn't help. If I wanted to get out of this, I'd have to rely on them. And that meant taking Mariner's place.

Only knowing what I did about the Syndicate, I'd never be able to try what Mariner had tried. I'd never get up enough nerve to run away and attempt to make money on my own. I'd just go on stooging forever—or until they decided they'd had enough.

I thought about it for the full hour. But long before the hour was up, I'd made my decision.

Finally, I walked back to their room and knocked on the door.

Miss Fairborn opened it. Her big eyes wide and luminous in welcome.

"All right," I said. "You win. But get me out of here, fast. I can't stand that body in there—"

She smiled. "Certainly. We've contacted our superiors and all arrangements have been made for you. Just check out of your room and stop worrying. Now, here're your orders . . ."

That was three weeks ago. Since then I've been to Detroit and Dallas and now I'm on my way to Kansas City. They gave me a new name—Lloyd Jones—and credentials to match. Everywhere I go, I am met by contacts who give me instructions. I make the investments and I sit in my hotel room. I can see where it's going to be an endless, monotonous grind.

But I can stand that part of it. It's just that lately, something else had started to worry me.

You see, I remember how I got on the trail of Mr. Mariner. I was ambitious; I wanted to find a man who had the secret of playing the market. So I looked around, and finally I found him. As a result, I was responsible for his death. At the very least, precipitated it.

No, it isn't my conscience that's bothering me.

It's this.

Somewhere, someplace, there must be others like myself—little guys with big ideas. And somewhere, sooner or later, another man is going to start looking for a fabulous character who seems to have the golden touch. He's going to run across my name, and he's going to make up his mind, like I did.

And then he'll come looking for me.

If he finds me—well, I remember only too well what happened to Mariner.

There's no sense trying to run; I'm trapped in my new identity. I can only wait until the man catches up with me. And, meanwhile, I'll keep on making millions. Doing what I always wanted to do—make a killing in the market.

But the next victim might very well be me.

Gone as by Magic
Richard Hardwick

WITH THE PASSAGE OF TIME—almost a year had gone by since Frank Pilcher disappeared as cleanly as if a space ship had dropped down and whisked him away, leaving not the slightest trace—Frank was emerging as something of a legend. The memory of him, man and boy, was slowly stripped of frailties and shortcomings, and his strong points were magnified and polished like fine hand-rubbed wood. At any gathering, from a cocktail party at one of the fashionable homes up on the Hill where Frank and Vera had lived, to a Saturday night brawl at Mel's bar out in the mill section, the talk eventually came round to Frank. He was the *Marie Celeste* of Garrison, the enigma in a town without enigmas, mystery in a prosaic place.

Some people thought of Frank as wandering aimlessly about somewhere, a victim of amnesia in a world with no past. There were those who said he was reclining happily beneath a palm this very minute in Tahiti or Pago Pago and hadn't the slightest notion of letting Vera or anyone else know where he was. A few, like Vera herself, said that Frank was dead. There was never a shred of proof to back up any of the theories. All they knew for certain was that he had disappeared one night, taking with him two suitcases containing certain items of clothing and toiletries, and nothing at all of a positive nature had been heard of him since.

Of course there were occurrences such as the time George Simpson swore he saw Frank in Atlanta, saw him walking along Broad Street as carefree as you please. Frank had ducked into a crowded drugstore and had given George the slip. But it had been Frank, of that George was certain.

There was a minority in Garrison, a minority of one, who did not have to theorize about Frank's disappearance. That was me, Burt Webb, and I knew where Frank was because I had dug the grave myself, laid him neatly in it, and covered him up.

I killed Frank intentionally, yet without any conscious premeditation. Why should I kill a man who was perhaps my best friend? I grew up with him, or rather, in his shadow. Frank was good at anything he chose to undertake, always a notch higher than I whether it be athletics, studies, social activities—anything at all. Yet, there is a pride of association that is felt in simply being identified with someone who is head and shoulders above the crowd, and it was this pride I felt. When it happened, I realized that I had hated Frank Pilcher nearly all my life. But if Frank had not done what he did, it's conceivable that both of us would have gone on to old age as friends.

If there was a weakness in Frank's makeup, a flaw in his structure, it was gambling. He would gamble on anything, for anything, with anybody. The two of us, for example, had a sort of running gin game. The stakes were moderately high, higher than I could afford if the truth were known, but the score went on, tipping once Frank's way and then mine. There was never any mention of a payoff. Until that night.

Vera was out of town. She and her mother had gone to New York on a shopping trip and Frank had been alone for several days. He called me at the office and I drove out after work. He was restive and quieter than was usual for him. Something seemed to be on his mind, some sort of decision. We had a few drinks and then Frank suggested we play gin. According to the total when we had last played, I owed Frank a little over fourteen hundred dollars.

From the first hand my luck ran badly, almost unbelievably so. By midnight I was in debt to Frank for more than twice the amount I had owed him at the start of the evening.

"To bad, Burt," he said as he spread his cards, once again, on the table. "Gin."

I threw my hand down and poured myself a stiff drink.

"It's the rottenest run of luck I ever saw!"

"When you came tonight I hoped you'd win. I feel like squaring accounts." He shuffled the cards idly. "Tell you what. Let's cut for the whole thing." Frank looked at the score pad, made a few calculations with his pencil. "It's fifty-four hundred. How about it?"

By his voice I sensed his excitement. "That's crazy," I said. "I can't afford what I already owe you!" It had never happened like this before. The pendulum always seemed to swing back. Insofar as skill went, we were about evenly matched, each knew the game the other played.

"If you can't afford it, you can square it with a cut of the cards."

"Or owe you ten thousand . . ."

"Ten thousand eight hundred," Frank grinned. He kept on riffling the cards. "If I didn't think you were good for it, Burt, I wouldn't gamble with you."

He was undoubtedly referring to an inheritance an aunt had left me a month or two before. What he didn't know was that that had been spoken for on several sides and was gone as soon as I got it.

I looked at the cards in his hands. Fifty-two little individuals, many of which could pull me out of a hole. If Frank cut a deuce, there were forty-eight left that would rescue me.

He passed them over to me. "Here, you shuffle them."

"I—I think I'd better call it a night, Frank. I've had a little more to drink than I should have . . ." But my hands were shuffling the cards and then the deck was lying there squared away between the two of us.

"Want me to take first cut?" Frank said.

I picked up my drink and took a deep swallow. "Go ahead."

He reached out, flexed his fingers, and lifted the top third of the deck. He turned it over slowly. He had cut the ten of diamonds. Frank put the cards back gently and folded his arms.

There were thirty-two losing cards there. Four to tie. Sixteen winners. That was all I could think of as I reached for the deck. I cut quickly, the way one will dive into cold water, because waiting merely makes it worse. I turned up the six of spades. I could hear myself breathing, feel Frank's amused stare.

"Maybe your luck'll change," he said.

"It's not luck!" I shouted. "You've done something to the cards! I've never had a streak like this before—"

"You're not accusing me of cheating, are you, Burt?" The amusement was gone from him now. He was cold.

"I don't know how—"

"Then don't make an accusation. Do you want to try to even it again? You owe me—"

"*Damn you!* I know how much it is!" I snatched up the deck and began to shuffle them violently. I shuffled them over and over, keeping my eyes on Frank the entire time. There was something different about him. He had the look of a man who was about to embark on something; he seemed filled with the impending excitement of a plane terminal or an ocean liner before departure. Or perhaps it was merely my own state of mind that exaggerated what I thought I saw.

I finished shuffling. "I'll cut first."

He nodded, and I took a breath and reached for the cards. I clamped my extended fingers down on the deck so that Frank would not see that they trembled. Once more I cut cleanly, quickly. The card I turned up was the queen of spades. The witch, we called her in heart games years ago.

I replaced the segment of the deck, realizing now my chances of coming out of this were excellent. Eight cards could top me, four—including the witch—tie. The deck held forty losers.

Frank remained composed, with only this inner excitement flickering in his eyes. "A king or an ace," he said, and he cut an ace. The ace of hearts.

My fist seemed to go across the table of its own volition. Frank still had the cards in his hand, the ace facing me when my blow caught him and sent him toppling backward. His head struck the floor with a resounding thump and I was across the table and on him before he could move. I saw my hands at his throat, and even then some flickering whisper deep inside me said to pull back. But the thumbs pressed down, pushing deep into the base of his throat.

It was a long while before my shaking muscles began to relax, and when they did, Frank Pilcher was far beyond any help on earth.

Frank was dead, and with him my debt. In its place I had an even worse problem. There'd be no explaining this away. You don't accidentally throttle the man people consider your best friend. I went to the sideboard and poured myself a stiff drink. The terrible range of emotion I had experienced left me drained of everything. The whiskey might as well have been a soda pop. I went about picking up the cards and then I sat down and counted them, glancing over at Frank's body every now and then and still feeling no remorse, no terror, only a sort of detached wonder. Perhaps those other emotions would come later. I had a desire to feel remorseful about Frank, for we had been friends for a long, long time. Outwardly, at least.

Now I had to think of myself. If I had been seen coming to Frank's, then I was lost. But the house was well hidden in a grove of trees; in this part of town privacy had been sought and paid for. I'd have to go ahead on the assumption that no one had seen me and that Frank had not mentioned my coming to anyone. Even at that it would be sticky going when they began to look for him.

I packed two of his suitcases with the logical things Frank would take if he were going on an extended trip and loaded them into my car. There was a deserted farm some miles from Garrison on which the company I worked for had foreclosed a few months earlier. At the time I had inspected the property, and it was here that I decided to bury Frank. I took one of the several shovels from his toolshed, checked the house to make certain there was no trace of the struggle or my visit, and then I locked the front door and drove away.

It rained in the early morning hours just before dawn, after I was home and in bed. The rain came slowly, almost reluctantly at first, and then as though some floodgate had been removed, it poured down in great windswept torrents.

I stood at the window and watched it slash against the pane. After the rain stopped, the day dawned gray and somber and solemn. It was the sort of day to make you think of eventual death.

Vera wore black from the first. I sat on the terrace with her and her mother, and from my seat I could clearly see the table just inside the sliding glass doors where Frank and I had played our last game. Vera looked very fine in black.

"He's dead. I know he's dead. Frank would never have gone off this way with no explanation, simply vanishing. He loved me, Burt. A woman knows those things."

"I can't understand all that lawyer was saying, Vera," her mother said in a whining voice.

"I should think," Vera said, "an idiot could have understood him. We're broke, dear. Frank left us a legacy of heavy mortgages and past due debts."

I was startled. "Do you mean there's—there's *nothing*? Out of all this, everything Frank built up, he accumulated nothing!"

"I'm no fool," Vera said bitterly. "I knew about Frank's gambling. The trips he took to Los Vegas and the other places. He told me time and again he would quit."

"Maybe that's why he left, because he couldn't quit—"

"He is dead." She flatly emphasized each word. "I know that because Frank would not have left me, not under any circumstance. He's been killed and I intend to find out who did it and where Frank's body is."

Guilt is a strange thing. I had the distinct feeling that Vera was looking into my mind, that she knew I had killed her husband and she was waiting patiently for me. There was a coldness inside me, even though I knew my secret was safe. A month had gone by since Frank's disappearance, and with each day that passed I felt my position was more secure. The first week was the ticklish one, never knowing when someone might come forward and point the finger at me and say, "Why, I remember now! I saw Burt Webb's car coming out of Frank's place after midnight," or "Frank mentioned to me that Burt was coming out that night." Such a statement would have been enough because I had no alibi.

Vera was saying, "There was one thing Frank tried to provide for and that was security for me. He had a great deal of life insurance. But the way it stands now, with no proof that he is dead, the insurance won't be settled for the required seven years."

"Vera, why would anyone want to kill Frank? He was one of the most liked and respected men in Garrison."

She shrugged. "Maybe he owed money he couldn't pay. Gambling debts. I understand they do things like that in order to discourage bad debts."

I began to feel an easing of the tension within me. She was thinking in terms of some sort of mob vengeance, cement shoes, that sort of thing. It was my own guilt focusing on itself that gave me the uneasiness.

"I think that lawyer was wrong," her mother said. "How will we live if we don't have money?" She smiled at Vera as though she had made a discovery.

Vera threw back her head and laughed. "Isn't that marvelous, Burt! Did you hear that? The lawyer's wrong because we have to *have* money to live! Now there's a classic bit of reasoning!"

I stood up, feeling ill at ease. "I've got to be going. Vera, if there's anything I can do . . . ?"

Vera went to the edge of the terrace. Her back was to me. "Find out who killed Frank, Burt. That's what you can do."

There was something about Vera's positive attitude that got under my skin. How could she be so certain Frank wouldn't have left her? What makes a woman presume that she knows a man, any more than a man can know a woman? They're like two entirely different species.

Years ago, I had been in love with Vera myself. She was the most beautiful girl in the crowd I grew up with. I suppose half the boys I knew were in love with Vera at one time or another, but it was different with me because in my senior year at high school I actually got encouragement from her. It was quite some time before I realized that

Vera was reaching Frank Pilcher through me, that I was a means to an end. Being a very stony character in those days, I shrugged it off and told myself it didn't matter because there were plenty more girls and, after all, Frank Pilcher was my best friend and it hadn't been Frank who did it but Vera. Vera was the calculating one. Frank was very apologetic about it, and I consoled him by saying it was just one of those things. It was all sophisticated and worldly, considering the three of us were seventeen years old at the time. I didn't want either of them to know how deeply I resented it, losing something else to Frank.

Frank was dead now, which certainly should even a lot of old scores. Vera said she was broke, though in seven years she would get his life insurance, which I gathered was a considerable amount. If I had been thinking of vengeance against Vera when I killed him, it had been so deeply buried in my subconscious that a platoon of psychiatrists couldn't have blasted it out. But when I left Vera that day, and saw that she was wearing black even though quite a few people were convinced Frank was not dead at all, but had run off, I knew I wanted to hurt her more. A death is a temporary hurt to those left behind, it is something that is inevitable. A betrayal, that is something else. If only Vera could be persuaded that Frank had betrayed her, then I would be pleased.

Paul Royce was one of the many people in Garrison who seemed to be trying to escape vicariously through Frank Pilcher. The ones who wanted to believe he had run off.

"Frank was putting money aside for years, you can bet on that," Royce told me one day. "People talk about his gambling, but that boy had a big income, a lot of property. You know what I think? I think he planned it just this way, disappearing like he did so nobody would know what happened to him. Sure, some of those professional gamblers could have killed him, but why would they do that? If Frank was broke, it wasn't like having some bum in the gutter owing you money. Frank could make it, and eventually he would have paid back every cent he owed. Did you notice how evenly balanced his estate came out? Every legitimate debt was paid in full, and no matter what Vera

Pilcher says, he left her an income that she can get along on. Frank's just as alive as you and me. No, I'd say he was *more* alive than you or me."

There're always those that want to get away. They don't seem to know what it is they want to get away from, it's just get away. To them Frank Pilcher had done just that and he was duty bound to be living somewhere the way a man should live.

It was the continual reference to this cache Frank was supposed to have had that held my interest. The months slipped by, three, four, and still you heard people talking about him. If Vera got wind of all the talk about Frank being in Tahiti or Paris or the Riviera or some other place, she never showed it. She still wore black in mourning for Frank, and I heard from someone that she had engaged a private investigator in her efforts to find out what had happened to her husband. I wondered if this persistence of hers was an effort to convince herself she was right.

The gambling luck I had the night I killed Frank clung to me like an albatross. Everything I touched turned to dust. Almost a year after Frank's death, the company I worked for closed their Garrison office and I was halfheartedly offered a lower position with another office. I refused the offer. Stocks I had carefully selected went steadily downward. I was, to put it euphemistically, hard-pressed.

And then I ran into Sid Vickers. Sid and Frank and I had been classmates. Sid's downhill slide had begun a long time ago, and when he approached me on the street that day, he had changed so that I didn't recognize him. He had always been a drab little fellow, the sort that tags along for any crumb that might be cast his way. He touched my sleeve and said, "It's me, Burt. Sid. Sid Vickers . . . ?" It was a question the way he said it, as though the name might very likely have lost all meaning for anyone other than himself. He was unshaven and dirty and terribly hungover.

"Could you let me have a couple of bucks, Burt? Just till I get on my feet . . . ?"

Almost everything I had was gone with the possible exception of my facade, and that was sagging. I looked at

Sid and wondered how long it would be before he and I would be indistinguishable.

"What is it you really want?" I asked him. "A drink?"

He smiled and began to laugh silently. "Never could fool you, Burt, could I? That's right, I need a drink. I need it bad."

There was a bar a couple of doors down. "I'll have one with you," I told him.

It wasn't much of a place, but we took a booth and I had two beers and a pint of blend brought over. Sid took a quick one, and then another. He leaned back in the booth and sighed gratefully. "Not like the old days, is it? Me and you and Frank Pilcher and the rest of the gang."

"No, Sid, it isn't like the old days." Everybody wanted to talk about Frank. Well, let them talk.

He poured another drink slowly. "Now, Frank Pilcher, there was a man. You know, I get a kick hearing everybody talking about Frank, guessing about him. Not me, though. I know what happened to him."

Suddenly, looking across the table into those bleary, puffy eyes, I wondered at the chance meeting outside on the street. Had I slipped up somewhere? There was the guilt again. I tried to retain my outward calm. I even managed what I hoped was an easy, slightly bored, smile.

"So you know where he is. You and half this town—"

"Oh, I didn't say *where*, Burt. I said I knew what happened to him. And there's a big difference because he could be anywhere, and I do mean anywhere. He had a pot put aside for his rainy day. Frank was my friend when nobody else was, except you, Burt. You always did treat me right, ever since I can remember. You're a friend if I ever had one in this world." He was belting the bottle steadily now.

"Sure, sure. I'm your friend, Sid. Now what's this about Frank?"

"Like I say, he had his pot put away at the end of the rainbow. I know because I saw it."

"You . . . you *saw* it?"

"I saw the key and he told me about it. The key to the safe deposit box where he had this dough stashed. There

was a little tag on the key with the name he used and the
way he had to sign to get into—"

"Why didn't you tell all this to someone during the investigation?"

"Nobody asked me," he said simply. "Come to think of
it, you didn't ask me either, did you?"

"That's all right. He was my friend and I'm interested in
knowing as much as I can about what happened to him."
This should bring a response that would tell me one way
or the other. "No key turned up—" That was almost a
slip, but Sid broke in.

"Sure it didn't!" Because he took it with him!"

But he hadn't taken it with him, because he hadn't gone
anywhere. No mysterious safe deposit key had turned up
among his effects, either. At least none that had led to a
box of cash.

"You're wondering why Frank would talk to me about
something like that, something he probably never told another soul. Well, I've wondered about it too, but I don't
think he even remembered doing it. Both of us were higher
than two kites at the time. I ran into him, just the way I
ran into you today, and we went to a bar and talked about
the good old days, you know how it is. It gets real foggy
about then, but I remember he had his wallet out to pay for
the booze and then he looked at me kind of funny and he
took this key out of the wallet and showed it to me. He told
me that was the key to the situation, or something like that."
Sid poured himself another drink. "So that's how I know
what happened to our old buddy, Frank Pilcher!"

I had buried Frank's wallet with him, and I hadn't looked
into it. I stared at Sid as he drank. I tried to read something
in that whiskey-swollen face. Was he making this up as a
sort of payment for the drinks I bought him? Was he
leading up to something else? Maybe Frank had told him
about my owing him money. But no, what possible connection could Sid make out of that and Frank's disappearance. Sid was telling me something that had actually happened to him. Frank *did* have a secret cache, something
Vera didn't know about, something he was keeping from
Vera. It made me want to laugh.

"This . . . this tag you say was on the key, what name was on it? Frank's?"

"What difference does it make? I don't think I read it, and even if I did I probably wouldn't have remembered it—"

"Yet you remember the key," I said quickly. "How is that?"

"Say, what's this all about. What's so important all of a sudden?"

I had become overly excited, was pressing too hard. "There's nothing sudden about it. Maybe you knew he didn't leave much behind for Vera—"

"Here's to sweet old Vera," he said, lifting his glass. Then I remembered little Sid was in love with Vera too, and she had never lowered herself to recognize his existence.

There was nothing to be gained by staying and watching Sid as he got drunk, so I left him. I wanted to think. This information of Sid's could be the answer to my problems. If there was a key there with Frank, and if it had a tag showing the assumed name he used and the way he signed it to gain access to the deposit box, what was there to prevent me from practicing that signature until I was able to duplicate it and go to the bank myself and get what was in the box? The bank's name would be on the key in all likelihood. He wouldn't have chosen a local bank for this; he would have gone somewhere, probably a large city, where he wasn't known. By now enough time would have passed so that there was a very good chance no one at that bank would recognize him. I could pass as the box-holder simply by signing the right signature and having the key in my possession.

That afternoon I went to see Vera, a friendly visit. The big house she and Frank and her mother had lived in had gone into the settlement of the estate, and had been sold. Vera now lived in a modest efficiency in a not-too-good section of Garrison. When she answered my ring I was amused to see she still wore black.

She offered me tea and after a few halfhearted amenities I began to get to the point which had brought me here. "There's still a lot of talk about Frank," I said. "Talk that says he had a lot of money put away somewhere—"

"I don't want to discuss it, Burt," she said, her eyes flashing. "He is dead. He loved me far too much to run out on me. As far as his money goes, Frank gambled it away and there's nothing that can be gained now by talk."

She was believing what she wanted to believe. "I hear you've got an investigator working for you," I went on.

She wasn't happy with me. "I can't see waiting another six and a half years to begin living like Frank wanted me to. If I can find out what happened to him, prove he's dead, then the life insurance claims will be paid."

"Frank was no stupid gambler. He was smart; he knew the odds when he played. I can't believe he would have lost everything—"

She stood up, her eyes narrowed. "If you don't mind, Burt, I don't feel well this afternoon. Perhaps you could call again some other time?"

Dismissed. But that was all right, because I knew there was doubt in Vera. I was pressing too logical an argument, one that she intuitively knew would do nothing more than shake her faith, so she put an end to it.

Her mother came in as I was leaving. She nodded absently at me and then spoke to Vera, the same old whine in her voice. "Have you heard anything from that detective, dear? He should have found out something by now. You're not harsh enough with him."

Vera's mother hadn't been weaned, as yet, from the good life.

I was unable to sleep. I was infected with a burning excitement now, thinking about the key I had buried with Frank. I lay in my bed like a kid on Christmas Eve, visualizing everything that was possible, wondering how much money Frank had socked away over the years. It occurred to me then that the night I killed him, Frank had actually been trying to let me off the hook. I remembered the way he put it. "I feel like squaring accounts," he'd said. He must have been planning then to make his exit before Vera came back from her trip.

Knowing Frank, his thoroughness, his ability, there

would certainly be a sufficient amount to see me through life in the manner to which I would like to be accustomed.

At last I slept, but not before memory recalled the old threat of Christmas, the promise of ashes if you weren't a good boy.

I was not entirely sure I had the stomach for what had to be done. I was a little old to be starting as a ghoul. But, there's no ghoul like an old ghoul. The next morning I drove out to the farm, which still remained unsold, as it likely would for a long, long time. I pulled my car around behind the tumbledown farmhouse, out of sight of anyone on the highway, and I went directly to the spot where I had buried Frank, some fifty yards from the house. At first I wasn't certain I had the exact spot, but I began to dig anyhow. I was in luck. About four feet down I reached him, a mouldering shoe, then a trouser leg in surprisingly good condition. The year had been an unusually dry one, which probably accounted for this.

I uncovered the body up to the waist; I had no desire to see its face. The wallet would be in the inside pocket of his coat, and I had reached that and had my fingers on the wallet and was in the act of pulling it out of the pocket when, suddenly, I stopped. I squatted there, stock-still, my head below the ground level. Yet, someone was gazing fixedly at the back of my neck; I felt someone's eyes on me.

"Don't try anything, Webb," a man's voice said. "Just hold everything right there where you are."

"I knew I was right!" This was Vera's voice. "I *knew* it! Now let's hear what all of them have to say about Frank! I knew he would never have left me!"

I didn't turn. I stared down at the wallet I held in my hand and I cursed myself for the most gullible of fools. I had fallen for a trick that was so patently a trap, a five-year-old would have spotted it. A baited trap, not subtly baited, but with a big sign and Klieg lights. Come and get it! Money, money, money! More than you can ever spend . . . !

Little Sid Vickers had sold out to the woman he hated, I

guessed, for the price of a bottle or two. There was no key. No money.

Feet rustled cautiously over the dry leafy ground. "All right," the man's voice said, "come on up out of there, and no funny business!"

I straightened slowly, the wallet in my hand. I turned and looked at them. The man I didn't recognize, but I assumed he was the detective Vera had hired. Vera's face mirrored her triumph. She made no effort to conceal the way she felt. She had kept Frank Pilcher to the end. Any doubt she may have secretly felt was gone now, as would be the doubts of others when the news was out. Her point was proven. All this time Frank had been less than five miles east of Garrison, and four feet straight down. Not in Tahiti or Paris or Pago Pago or anywhere, but on an abandoned farm in a crude grave.

I hated her then more than I ever hated anyone. Not so much for trapping me—that had been due to my own gullibility—but for getting her proof.

"I knew you had something to do with this," she said. "You tried harder than anyone else to make me think Frank had left me. I had you followed, Burt. When Pierce saw you come here and start digging, he came back and got me. He knew I'd want to be here in person to see how you take it!"

"Well, Vera, your trap with Sid worked."

No affirmation. Suddenly, I began to wonder. I looked down at the wallet, and slowly I opened it. "What are you doing there, Webb?" the detective said menacingly, waving his gun. I paid him no heed, but pulled the cards and papers out of the wallet, letting them all drop until I found what I was looking for. A key, and a tag with a stranger's name attached to it.

I was smiling bitterly when I tossed it to Vera.

The Big Bajoor
Borden Deal

VANYA HURRIED DOWN the side of the highway to the place where the trailer was parked. The trailer was pulled off the side of a road into a small clearing. When she stepped across the ditch, she saw Sandor lying on his back under the nearest tree. He had his fiddle in his hand, but he was not playing.

Vanya stopped to look at Sandor from a distance, before he should be aware of her presence. He was a Rom any gypsy girl could be proud of loving. He was tall, handsome, his black hair curled about his ears, and he played the fiddle as the old ones had played it. Vanya herself was small, dark, pretty; but she had never expected to capture such a Rom as this one. Watching him, she felt the old familiar stab of love and pride inside her.

She came on, then, and Sandor looked up to watch her approach. He scowled, slightly, and she knew that he had planned the scowl for her appearance.

"Well, Vanya," he said. "Are you through dukkering? It was yesterday that I wanted to coor the drom and get started traveling."

"We can travel tomorrow," Vanya said breathlessly. "Today is the day for telling fortunes."

"So how much money did you make?" Sandor said indifferently.

"None," she said. She saw the frown again between his black eyes and she hastened with the news. "But I've got a big bajoor."

Sandor sat up. Vanya watched him with pride and joy. For a year, now, they had been married and she had not had a big bajoor. Every good wife makes the big bajoor for her Romany husband. Without the big bajoor she was not a good wife; and for a year now Vanya had not found it.

"Boro Dad!" Sandor said, his voice tense with the excitement. "You don't mean to say. Who are we going to swindle?"

Vanya sat on the ground beside Sandor. She took off her kerchief and loosened her hair to cool the heat from her head. "There's an old gajo woman who lives up the road," she said. "Yesterday I stopped for a drink of water. She lives in a big house just on the edge of the town, a house that was painted twenty years ago. It has seventeen rooms and it sits on a very large lot. The old woman lives there alone."

"So?" Sandor said impatiently.

"So today I stopped again. Today I told her fortune. She believed the fortune, for more than an hour I had to tell her all the bad she has seen and all the good that she will see. She is a very lonely old lady."

"She's probably got next week's grocery money," Sandor said. "This is a big bajoor?" But his eyes were sparkling with the excitement and the smile was in them that was not on his lips.

"I told her that I was a queen of the gypsies," Vanya said. "I told her I had the power to bless money in such a way that would keep it safe and increase it by as much again. The old gajo woman believed. I could tell that she believed."

Vanya turned to Sandor, put her hand on his arm. She squeezed the arm tightly. "She showed me the money, Sandor. She opened the trunk to show me this great bundle, wrapped in newspapers and tied with string. I told her I would prepare the magic and this afternoon I would bless the money for her, because she was a kind lady who gives a gypsy a drink of water."

Sandor grinned. He loved Vanya. But it is good for a man to be proud of his wife, too. He could hear himself now, telling the story of the big bajoor and how his lovely young wife had worked it.

"The old gypsy switch," he said.

Vanya nodded her head. "Yes," she said.

He frowned uncertainly. "Can you work it?" he said. "Have you ever tried?"

Vanya drew herself straight. "My mother worked a great bajoor," she said. "Ten thousand dollars for my father. In one day."

He grinned ruefully. "Don't I know it? That's all I heard about when I set out to buy you from your father. It raised your price nearly out of my range."

She touched him again. "I will work the big bajoor," she said. "Or I will not come back."

She went then to prepare the meal. While she worked she sang, because she was so full of the happiness she had found today. She knew that her price had been high and she knew that Sandor loved her for he had paid a great deal of money for her. And until now she had made them only a living, nothing more.

They sat on the ground and ate companionably of the noon meal. They did not speak of the swindle again. After the meal would be soon enough. When the meal was finished, they went silently to work to prepare. Sandor helped her with the preparations. He drove into town and bought two reams of white paper and an ample supply of newspapers. They cut the white paper into dollar-sized pieces, stacking them carefully, Vanya measuring the stack from time to time with her hands.

"That's about the size of the bundle she had," she said at last.

"Then your daughters will be old maids," he said, laughing. "For no Romany will be able to afford them."

She laughed with him, tasting the sheer happiness in the sound of his voice, and together they wrapped the bundle in newspaper and tied it with the red string. She went into the trailer and changed into the dress with ampler folds, and put on the cloak over it. She wrapped up some of the leftover newspaper with a supply of the red string, and put the incense into a pocket of the dress.

She came outside again and picked up the bundle of blank paper wrapped in the newspaper and tied with the red string.

"Can you handle it all right?" Sandor said anxiously. "It's a pretty big bundle."

"I can handle it," she said confidently. She smiled at him and her hands moved quickly, concealing the bundle inside the voluminous dress. "See?"

"But the switch . . ."

She laughed. "Don't worry, Sandor," she said. "I can make the switch. I am the daughter of my mother, and I am Sandor's wife."

"I will be ready," he called after her as she started toward the road. "We will leave as soon as you return."

She tried not to hurry. But she was anxious for the deed to be accomplished, to have it a fact of her life that she had made a bajoor bigger than her mother had ever done. There was the love of Sandor and the thirst for fame strong in her throat and both were urging her on in spite of the flutter of fear deep down in her stomach. Vanya was young, only twenty, and her mother had been already old when she had accomplished her great feat.

There was nothing to arouse her suspicions. Everything looked as it had this morning. She entered between the old broken concrete gateposts and went up the walk. She stopped on the porch and the door opened immediately without her knock.

She looked at the woman standing in the doorway. She was tall, spare, with a large nose. Her hair was white, and once, you could tell, she had stood erectly. But now her shoulders were stooped.

"I have come," Vanya said in an impressive voice.

"I followed your instructions," the old lady said, her voice whispering. "You must bless my money. You must keep it safe."

"And double it," Vanya said.

"I don't care about doubling it," the old woman said. "But I must keep it, for if I don't I could never face my father again."

Vanya had started for the room where she had told the fortune this morning. Now she stopped, turned.

"Your father?" she said. "Is he . . . ?"

"He is dead," the old lady said. "If I lost the money I would even be afraid to die."

Vanya went on, followed by the old lady. She went into the room and looked about her. It was the same as this morning, cool, high-ceilinged, dusky with darkness from the thick drawn drapes in spite of the great sunlight outside. No preparation of the room would be necessary.

There was a chair before a table and the old lady had placed the bundle of money, wrapped in tattered newspaper, on the table.

"Sit in the chair," Vanya said.

The old lady sat down. Vanya lit the incense and placed it on the table. The fragrant sweet smoke billowed up into the room, making the old lady blink her eyes. Vanya spoke some words in Calo, the gypsy tongue, reverberating them with her diaphragm so that they echoed in the room.

"Now," she said. "Take this newspaper and this red string and wrap your money carefully. Tie it with many knots."

The old lady took the newspaper and string uncertainly, with trembling hands. "I have arthritis," she said. "You will have to wrap it and tie it."

Vanya drew back in horror. "No," she said. "I cannot touch the money. If I touched the money while I was blessing it, I would die."

She began chanting in Calo while the old lady began to prepare the bundle with the newspaper and the red string. She was slow and uncertain but Vanya pushed down the impatience that rose within her.

"You are so kind," the old lady said. "No one has been kind to me for so long. Nobody comes here any more, you know. People used to come here. Before the War between the States they held great dances here. People still came in my father's time. But they don't come any more."

"When you are kind to a gypsy, great blessings come into your life," Vanya said. "For this reason I bless your money."

"I want to pay you, though," the old lady said. "I have five dollars right here to pay you with."

"I cannot take pay for the blessing of money," Vanya

said. "This is a thing that gypsies do only for friends, and from a friend a gypsy cannot take money."

Vanya did not let herself think about the old woman and her loneliness and her money. She kept herself thinking about Sandor instead, and how much more he would love her now, and be proud of her. The woman was a gajo, wasn't she?

At last she was finished. The bundle sat on the table in the gloominess of the room. The room was filled with incense now, making it hard to see, the incense overwhelming the mind as well as the senses.

"Now," Vanya said. "You must close your eyes, for no one may look upon the blessing. To look upon the blessing would strike your mind, for it is a terrible and a hurting thing."

She watched closely to see if the old lady obeyed her. The eyes were tightly closed, the hands held stiffly in the lap, clenched into fists.

Vanya began chanting in Calo. She started low and far away, began coming nearer and louder, her body beginning to thump and beat against the sound of the voice. Her legs jerked out from under her and she thumped to the floor, where she thrashed, uttering terrible cries. She inched her way toward the table, making the sounds and watching the old lady. Not once did she look toward the table as her hand took out the fake bundle and held it ready. The eyes were closed. Swiftly, soundlessly, she switched the bundle, keeping up the thump and bang of her body against the floor while she edged away from the table. When she had reached her place, she began to let the terrible sounds subside, going gradually away into the distance until she lay silent.

At last she sat up and said, "You may open your eyes."

The old lady looked at her and Vanya stood up, wearily, making her face vacant and drawn.

"I have blessed the money," she said in a dull voice. "I have made it safe and it will double within three months. You must put it away into your keeping place and speak of it to no one. At the end of three months you may open it and see the increase my magic has brought you."

"Are you all right?" the old lady said, peering at her. "You look . . ."

"I must sleep for twenty-four hours," Vanya said in the weary voice. "Then I shall recover my strength. Gypsy magic is very strong. Remember. You must not look at the money. You must not speak of the money. Or the magic will be destroyed."

The old lady followed her as Vanya edged toward the door, anxious to be gone. "It worked all right?" she said anxiously. "It will be safe? My father gave the money to me, just like his father gave it to him."

"The magic worked," Vanya said. "I must go. I must sleep. I will be very ill, perhaps even die, if I do not sleep soon."

She got to the doorway, but the old lady was right behind her. The old lady put her hand on her arm. "You're sure it's all right?" she said.

"Of course it's all right," Vanya said, her voice cracking with the strain.

"Maybe we'd better look," the old lady said, her voice getting frenzied. She started toward the table where the package lay.

Vanya froze, watching her. Then her voice snaked out at her. "No," she said. "Not for three months."

The old lady turned to look at her and Vanya knew that she was suspicious now. It had risen up in her suddenly at the thought of the three months without seeing the money.

"I've got to be sure," the old lady said. "I don't care whether it doubles or not. That part doesn't matter. But it must be safe. I'll look. Then it'll be safe, even if it won't double . . ."

Already she was fumbling with the string. Vanya felt an impulse to flee. But she knew it would be wrong. That would certainly arouse the old lady. She stood with her hand on the doorknob, not knowing what to do, thinking, *I tried it too soon. I am too young for the big bajoor.*

The old lady's impatient hands ripped the newspaper and the white paper showed beneath. She looked toward Vanya, clutching a dollar-sized sheet of paper.

"What have you done with the money?" she screamed.

She came toward Vanya, almost running, clutching at her with both hands. Vanya, panicked, wheeled toward her, pushing her away, thinking now only of escape. She still had the money. If she could escape . . .

The old lady fell backward, clawing at the air. She made a strange cry when she landed on the floor, and there was in her an immediate limpness that frightened Vanya. She stood holding the door, looking down at the old woman, who lay twisted in a strangely familiar way.

At last Vanya left the door. She stood over the old lady, then she knelt down and put her hand on her face. "Mullah," she whispered. "Dead. Dead."

She squatted beside the old woman's body. It had been such a little push. But the old gajo woman had been so old. She knelt there, feeling the disaster that had come upon her in her youthful pride. She was no good for Sandor, no good for herself. She scarcely deserved to be called by the name Romany.

After a time, how long she did not know, she began to think more calmly. She still had the money, didn't she? She could hide the other bundle, clear away the incense and the other signs of a gypsy presence, and go away. The old lady lived alone. When she was found everyone would assume that she had fallen. She *had* fallen. Vanya had given her only a little push.

Vanya cleared the table of the incense holder, looked about the room. She didn't know what to do with the fake bundle. She picked it up, then, and took it to the chest where the old lady had kept her money. She put the bundle inside the chest, under a quilt, and locked the chest door. Let her relatives figure out why the old lady kept a bundle of paper tied up in newspaper and red string.

She went to the door and looked out carefully. Nothing stirred. She walked out on the porch, turned once and waved back toward the house as though speaking farewell to the old lady, and then went casually toward the highway. She made herself go slowly down the highway until she had covered more than a mile. Then she began to hurry.

She would not tell Sandor. She would tell him only that

the big bajoor had worked, that she had the money. He need not know how she had failed. No one would ever know that the old lady had fallen.

When she arrived, Sandor was ready. She got into the car beside him and immediately Sandor pulled into the highway.

"Did you get it?" he said briefly.

"Yes," she said, taking the bundle out of the voluminous dress and putting it on the seat between them.

They drove for a long time. At first Vanya slept, for she was weary, but when she awoke they were very gay. They laughed and sang and Vanya was warm with his love and with the coming fame of the big bajoor when their people should be told the story.

They did not stop until daylight.

"Time for breakfast, little one," Sandor said tenderly. He put his hand on her head and tousled her gently. "But first . . . let's look at our fortune."

His lean strong fingers began to undo the red string. Vanya watched him, not looking down at the money but watching his face as he saw it for the first time. She saw the change in him and her mind could not understand it. At last he looked up at her and his voice was strange when he spoke.

"Well, little Vanya," he said. "We're rich now. We're rich—just as soon as the Confederate States of America come back into power."

Vanya looked, then. She saw the bundle of carefully preserved Confederate bills, large and strange-looking, and she felt her soul curl inside her.

Sandor had never punished her, as gypsy men punish their wives. But she knew that he was going to do it now. Her mind revolted. She had killed the old woman and then the big bajoor had been a swindle on her instead. But her body did not move as she waited for Sandor to begin.

There was a silence. Then he opened the door of the car on his side. "Get out," he said. "Build a fire."

She got out of the car and went around to his side. She kept her eyes to the ground. He did not touch her.

"Build a fire," he repeated. "I want my breakfast, woman."

"Sandor," she said.

There was no pleading, no tears, in the voice.

"You are going to cook breakfast with the heat of your great bajoor," Sandor said above her.

She went away from him, began gathering the dry pine limbs. She moved numbly, as though she were an old woman. Sandor stood still, watching her as she knelt before the pile of sticks. He threw a match at her feet. Dazed, she struck it.

"A bigger fire," Sandor said.

She piled on the limbs she had brought. With one foot he kicked the package of Confederate money near her. Her hands tore the bills out of the stacks. She stopped, then.

"I can't burn money," she said. "Not even . . ."

"Burn it," he said.

She began putting the bills into the resin-hot fire. The flames licked at them, curling the edges, wisping them into ashes that preserved still the engraved pictures. She fed the fire steadily with the bills, her hands moving with a slow hurt that came from deep within her. It was a greater punishment than a beating from his broad leather belt.

Sandor went away, came back with the utensils for cooking. He dropped them by her side. "You have swindled me a great breakfast fire," he said. "See now if you remember how to cook my breakfast."

She put in the last handful of bills, scrabbled in the old newspaper to see if there were more. She picked up the thin booklet that had lain under the bills, hidden by them, and looked at it stupidly. It fell open in her hands. She kept on looking at it, laughing, a laughing that sounded like crying.

Sandor came back to her side, his face angrier still. "What's the matter with you, stupid woman?" he said.

She looked up at him, for the first time. She thrust the booklet toward him. "Look," she said. "Look. Where she has made the mark with the pencil."

He looked. His face turned white. He stalked away from

her toward the car. She looked at the booklet again, seeing where the old woman had marked the page.

"This money catalogue is old too," she called after him. "Yet here they are worth seventeen dollars apiece. Bodo Dad alone knows how much they are worth now."

He was gone into the trailer. She stood up shouting after him. "The father of the gajo woman was wise," she shouted after him. "He told the truth when he told her never to let it go. And you burned it. You burned my big bajoor. Seventeen dollars apiece!"

There was only silence. The anger and the weeping laughter left her. She squatted again beside the fire and looked into its red heart. She could still see the ashy outline of the last bill. She touched it with a stick and the ash crumbled so that it could not be distinguished from the rest.

She added the rare-money catalogue to the flames. Then she began cooking breakfast for her Romany man.

The Gentle Miss Bluebeard
Nedra Tyre

MISS MARY ANNE BEARD was not of a reflective or probing disposition, and so it did not occur to her to dwell upon how she had developed into a murderer. A talent for murders of a discreet and delicate nature came upon her unexpectedly in early old age, a gift full-blown and quite successful. Her prowess indicated that she might have been born to do murder.

If she had been compelled to form an opinion about her connection with murder, she very likely would have said she had fallen into it for lack of anything better to do. But she would not have been offhand about it. "Pride" seems a bizarre word to use as descriptive of the attitude she took toward her proficiency, and it lacks accuracy; yet she did regard her gift, her knack, her faculty—whatever it might be termed—with feeling approaching pride and wonder.

Her aptitude for murder first showed itself six months after her sixty-fifth birthday. It was then that she murdered for the first time. Her wits were about her; her purpose was clear, and she did not waver. That night after she had committed murder she slept well, remorse was not even a remote bedfellow. Two days later, wearing her best dress and newest hat, she went to her victim's funeral, not to gloat over her success, but out of respect to the dead man, of whom she was fond; she nodded toward his wife, muttered some apt words of unfelt sympathy, and listened with reverence to the service for the dead. Though the deceased was only an acquaintance, she was gratified that she had gone to the funeral because few people were there, her victim was old and had been bedridden for years, his friends had dropped away, and a shrew of a wife was his only relative.

Miss Beard murdered because there was not much else to do in her retirement: the paucity of her social-security check did not allow for other indulgences. That sounds

callous. It is not meant to be; for Miss Beard followed her
new calling with high resolve and dedication.

There was not much else that would have attracted her.
Actually, she had no taste for travel, even if she had had
the money for it.

Most of her previous leisure during her business career
had been devoted to reading. There had never been enough
time to do all the reading she wanted to do. Now that there
was time her sight had begun to fail; reading closed her
lids like a soporific, or else the print danced before her
eyes in some intricate ballet which she was unable to follow.

So reading was out.

For a short while to try to find something of interest
Miss Beard sought out the old-age clubs. The members at
these clubs were all pleasant enough, but Miss Beard resented being lumped with them for the sole reason that
they were all elderly. She did not feel an automatic member
of the aging, just because she had gotten up every day
that presented itself and had lived through it the best way
she could, and so by this natural and inevitable course had
accumulated an impressive number of years. No, she could
not identify herself with all these people. And so old-age
club activities were out, along with travel and reading.

So, in a sense, because there was nothing better to do in
the time of her retirement, Miss Beard took to murder.

She was modest about this gift; she must have nurtured
it through the years to have become suddenly so adept at
it, yet she had not once suspected this deadly and deathly
trait in herself. And then the long tunnel of memory bored
deep into her subconscious and she remembered that year
in the third grade when the children had taken up the
taunt, aping a boy—a mean, spiteful youngster—as he
called after her, *Mary Anne Beard, Mary Anne Bluebeard,
Bluebeard Mary Anne,* and after that many of the children
out of the teacher's hearing had called her Mary Anne
Bluebeard. But this name-calling had ended when her father
died and her mother moved to a more modest neighborhood
and Mary Anne had gone to another school, so that she and
her former classmates had been lost to each other in the
city's vastness. The name Bluebeard had hurt as it had

been meant to hurt, yet she had forgotten it until the time of her first murder. Her talent for murder had been dormant all those years and it might very well have been that the little boy—what was his name?—something simple —she had no head for names—had been gifted with unusual intuition and had divined her true nature. Anyway, her ease and adeptness at murder sometimes amazed her.

What amazed her even more was the number of people eager for death. She had believed that, however hazardous and fraught with discontent and discomfort existence might be, people still grasped at life. It was not so. Her victims were all obsessed with the death wish. The slightest gesture in death's direction and they embraced it like a lover. She learned with astonishment that a person needs only the tiniest encouragement—only a word, a gesture, or the slightest push or shove—when he or she is inclined toward death.

Her first victim's name was Smith, John Smith, and his life was as noncommittal as his name. Miss Beard had been as unaware of him as she was of the other tenants in the modest apartment house where she lived. It was a neighborly deed on her part, an offer to help in an emergency, that introduced them to each other; on their first meeting, there was no hint that their brief acquaintance would end in murder.

That afternoon Miss Beard heard the doorbells ring, the ringing progressed up one side of a corridor and down the other side. The walls of the apartments were thin, the bells sharp; it was a sound she had become accustomed to since her retirement—solicitors, salesman of one kind of another, making their rounds, neglecting no one, going from apartment to apartment, seldom getting an answer because it was a domicile of working people. The sound of steps approached and diminished, with the spitting buzz of the bells blaring in between. Her turn came. She answered the door. A woman flushed by irritation stood there. "I've got to leave the house," she said, "and the man who promised to come stay with my husband just phoned he can't come. I must go. It's urgent. Can you come?"

There was nothing tentative about the request; it was a

command. "Of course," Miss Beard said, as if the question were politely put, "I'll be glad to come."

And so she was admitted to the presence of her first victim: to Mr. John Smith. He lay there on the bed, a captive of heart disease.

Mrs. Smith barked an introduction to them and then busied herself in a bluster of leavetaking. The apartment was a glory of silence when she left, and then Miss Beard turned to Mr. Smith. From his bleak dominion he summoned up a smile for her. She answered him with a smile but could think of nothing to say, nor could Mr. Smith, who was like a timid child suffering a bad case of the cat had got his tongue, and so they smiled again at each other, and this exchange sealed their goodwill.

Miss Beard sat there as she was to sit on succeeding occasions when Mrs. Smith went to play bridge (cardplaying was the emergency that took her away, not anything more urgent than that) and she habitually called upon Miss Beard to sit with Mr. Smith, as Miss Beard came willingly and would accept no pay, whereas the man had to be cajoled into coming and charged a dollar an hour.

Though the total of their meetings were mounting at the rate of two a week, Miss Beard and Mr. Smith still found nothing to say to each other. Miss Beard was alert to any wish of his—his eyes glancing toward the water and she was up quickly to hand the glass to him, or a flicker of pain across his brow and she proffered a pill, and sometimes just to show her interest and concern, she would raise or lower the shade, tuck the blanket in, or remove it—and his smile would tender his gratitude. No words were spoken. He had come to mistrust words and spoken communication, and well he might, Miss Beard thought. For even during her brief stays in Mrs. Smith's presence, she had noticed the continuous barrage of Mrs. Smith's words directed against Mr. Smith. Once or twice when he had attempted an answer, Mrs. Smith had distorted what he said, a simple statement that she was not to worry he was in Miss Beard's good hands would be caught as if it were a barb and shot back at him with an arrow's speed to wound and hurt and make him cringe beneath the covers.

Then after the miracle of her departure, Miss Beard and Mr. Smith did not defile the blessed silence. Yet they had begun to plot and what they plotted was Mr. Smith's death. Those two gentle people began to collaborate on a deed of violence. No word was spoken; it was tacit planning.

There was the afternoon when Miss Beard had stolen for the first time in her life. Her theft was a rose for Mr. Smith. She had come back from the grocery store and there the rose was, leaning over a fence, tempting her; a thorn pricked her finger when she reached toward the vine, but that did not deter her in breaking off the blossom. It was the loveliest rose she had ever seen, and Mr. Smith's look of pleasure told her he thought so too when she handed it to him shyly. Though Mrs. Smith had been engrossed in dressing, her witch's heart had intuited something; she came to the door and saw Mr. Smith in the act of accepting the rose. "My, my," she said. "Nobody knows what goes on around here while I'm away." Her voice was a mockery, a taunt; nothing could possibly take place in her absence and she knew it.

And Miss Beard, aware that she was in the presence of an inquisitor, a sadist and tormenter, said to herself: Mr. Smith must get out of this at once. I must murder him right away, and Mr. Smith looked longingly at her, as if to answer, yes, you must, I can't endure this any longer.

Events proved immediately favorable; there was no need to dillydally.

That afternoon Mr. Smith had one of his attacks, and Miss Beard reached for the dosage Mrs. Smith had measured out, just in case. Miss Beard extended the glass, and in the midst of pain Mr. Smith looked at her and his lids blinked negatively, and she had taken the glass and poured the medicine down the lavatory. It would have done her no good to have had any remorse later and to have tried to replenish the glass, because she did not know from what bottle the medicine had been poured and the chest's shelves were regimented with bottles. She did not know Mr. Smith's doctor's name and so could not telephone him. Twice she tried to telephone the city hospital, but got only a busy signal. If there had been an answer she would have

asked for emergency service, but she might have given an
incorrect address, only to call later with a mild reproof
over the fact that the ambulance had not appeared. Anyway, it would have been too late.

Her second murder was something like trying out a new
recipe, wondering if it would work. Yes, it was like reading
a recipe and deciding to follow it sometimes if the ingredients were available. It came about in this way.

The house next door was very close and the people
living in the upstairs apartment opposite Miss Beard's used
loud voices in their anger. A lovely girl whose lovely face
was twisted into a hag's mask, shouted: "But Mama, has it
ever occurred to you that you have these attacks only when
I'm going out with Joe?"

The older woman answered: "It's no pleasure for me to
suffer alone here in this grubby apartment day in and day
out and then have you come home at night and scream at
me and rush out, just when I've been hoping we could have
a nice evening together."

"But, Mama, it's only once a week. Joe knows I have to
stay with you every night but one."

"Last week it was Friday and tonight's only Tuesday. Is
that once a week?"

And then Miss Beard watched the girl go to the telephone.
The voice she used was the cold, bitter one of women who
give up men or have been given up by them. For a long
time, the girl listened to the reply she had provoked and at
last said: "That's how it is, Joe. There's nothing I can do
about it." So for the second time, murder was to prove an
easy task for Miss Beard.

The next morning she watched the girl leave the apartment. Miss Beard joined her at the bus stop, and opened the
conversation with a reference to the weather gambit, then
sat down with the girl on the bus. The ride was not long,
but it took no time at all for the heartbroken girl to spill
out her despair to a sympathetic listener.

So it came about that instead of husband-sitting as in
Mr. Smith's case, Miss Beard began to mother-sit while the
girl went on dates with Joe. The woman, whose name was
Brown, enjoyed Miss Beard's company and her many

attentions—Miss Beard dearly loved to pamper people: a massage, a manicure, a shampoo, a cologne foot bath, an alcohol rub, pleasant conversation that lulled Mrs. Brown into sleep. Her last speech before she dozed off was invariably: "If Anne should leave me to marry Joe, I'll kill myself."

That was when Miss Beard decided to do it for her.

And yet Miss Beard was not sure just how this murder might be consummated, though she knew the deed must be done immediately, for Anne had whispered: "Joe asked me to marry him. I said yes. I don't know how to tell Mama. Help me to think of a way." And Miss Beard promised she would put on her thinking cap and try to figure out a way to break the news.

As it turned out, there was not a great deal to it. That next night Mrs. Brown complained of being chilly and asked Miss Beard to hand her a bed jacket. "It's just come from the cleaners," she said. "You'll find it in a plastic bag."

Miss Beard handed bag and all to Mrs. Brown. She watched Mrs. Brown take the jacket out and put it on and fling the plastic bag to the foot of her bed. Miss Beard talked on and on to her in her most soothing voice, and then after awhile the woman's resounding snoring began. There was nothing, Mrs. Brown had bragged, that could wake her once she had fallen asleep. It was then Miss Beard recalled what she had read in the newspapers, so many unfortunate cases recently of persons, usually babies or young children, being suffocated by plastic bags. It was really hard to believe they were so lethal. Miss Beard had not seen one before; her cleaners used old-fashioned paper bags. She wondered if plastic bags were as deadly as all that. Would it work? Ought she to try it? She might as well see if all those news stories had any truth in them. Surely it was worth a try. She picked the bag up from the foot of the bed and laid it across the edge of Mrs. Brown's pillow. Just then Mrs. Brown turned over in her sleep and burrowed deeply into the plastic bag.

Miss Beard tiptoed out.

She was not invited to the wedding; it was a small, very

private affair, coming so soon after a death in the family, only the closest friends and relatives were asked and Miss Beard was not among that group; she did send a present: two dessert spoons in Anne's pattern—Greenbrier.

Miss Beard encountered her third victim in the grocery store. The weather that day was perfect, the wind just right, the sun just warm enough; it did not seem possible to Miss Beard that there could be misery anywhere. But her awareness of sinister reality came back when she reached for a number two can of beets and turned to see a rapacious hand stretched toward the section marked Disinfectants. The hand belonged to a woman whose face was wracked and devastated by unhappiness; in the distraught eyes was a bald and bold lust for death.

Miss Beard, thinking only of the woman's suffering, and not of her own gift for murder, said: "My dear, you must sit down. Let's go to the drugstore next door. A sip of tea will help you."

Over the tea, the woman poured out such a pathetic account of betrayal that Miss Beard saw at once something must be done to try to comfort her. The tea grew tepid, and the tea bags, limp against the saucers, only added to the air of dismay and ruin. Something had to be done at once, the woman must not be allowed to commit suicide in the awful way she had planned, with poison causing slow, infernal pain and distortion and disfigurement.

The woman pleaded in a pathetic tone: "Do you mind walking home with me? I don't think I could cross a street without help."

"Of course, my dear, I'll be delighted."

And with Miss Beard's two shopping bags full of groceries and the woman's sack with its solitary fatal content, they walked to the dingy rooming house where the woman lived.

Inside, down labyrinthine halls filled with musty odors of days old cooking, the woman guided Miss Beard to a furnished room. The bed with its imprint of the woman's body, the pillow moist with her tears, the sink filled with coffee cups ringed with stains and grounds, the cheapness and shabbiness of everything, the solitary armchair with its stuffings bursting through, like some picador's injured horse whose belly had been ripped by a bull's horns, and the ceiling cracked and discolored, were too much for Miss Beard. All these evidences and echoes of misery were beyond her endurance.

The woman's teeth began to chatter, making hallow staccato sounds of grief.

"You must get in bed," Miss Beard urged. "You must warm yourself."

Miss Beard turned on the gas heater, and the heat made the exhausted woman relax. Miss Beard tucked her into the rumpled covers, and almost at once the woman fell asleep. Then Miss Beard saw the suicide note the woman had written earlier; it was stuck into the cracked mirror of the dresser. The woman's heavy breathing reassured Miss Beard; the room grew warmer and Miss Beard turned down the gas, and then she turned it off. The woman slept on and on and Miss Beard felt that she must leave. But the woman must not be allowed to wake in that dreary room with the newly bought disinfectant so conveniently at hand. There was a much easier way to carry off the whole thing.

Miss Beard turned the gas on. But she did not light it. She tucked towels at the window. The door fit snugly enough. The room was small; there was no reason why the gas should not take effect in a short time, and there was the suicide note to explain everything. Miss Beard had kept on her gloves—she had always worn gloves when she went out and when she worked around the house, strange that all her life she had prepared herself for a murderer's necessary precaution. Miss Beard picked up her shopping bags and left the woman's room.

She had forgotten how perfect the day was, until she walked out into the sunlight again.

As for her next murder, Miss Beard eased her fourth victim across death's threshold with a slight push, down a fire escape. And her fifth murder—no, her sixth—also involved a tiny push, this time down an embankment. Her seventh was an administering of an overdose of sleeping pills. And so they mounted: her eighth, ninth, tenth, eleventh and twelfth murders. She was most especially careful about her thirteenth—no matter how much anyone protests, every one is superstitious about the number thirteen.

And so it went, murder only slightly premeditated—one after the other, with no malice, and no such maudlin emotion as regret; murder in these instances seemed required and Miss Beard did not flinch; she felt no sorrow for what she had done and the persons she murdered benefited from her action.

There were no complications at all, though every now and again after her fourteenth endeavor she would have a strange, somewhat unsettling sensation that she was being watched, yet no one could possibly be watching her. What could any of those deaths mean to anyone living—all her victims had been emotional outcasts, no one had taken any notice of them except to wish them out of the way. Still the feeling of being watched persisted, and in an eerie fashion she half-expected the little boy whose name she had not been able to recall to dart out at her in some dim hall and shout, *Bluebeard Mary Anne, old Mary Anne Bluebeard*, and then to chant, *I told you so, I told you so, I've always known you were a murderer.*

One afternoon, after her fifteenth murder, the impression of being watched was so overwhelming she decided she needed a rest, her trouble must be that she had grown fidgety from overwork. Besides, all the chores were getting behind in her apartment. She should soft-pedal the murders for awhile; she had been overdoing them, zeal was triumphing over zest and that would never do. One or two crimes a month were all that she should reasonably expect of herself, whereas that last week she had disposed of three poor wretches.

A change of pace did prove helpful. She enjoyed her vacation from murder. Tidying, dusting, cleaning out drawers, puttering around, shifting furniture were most satisfying. And then time began to pall; she must get her hand back in; that poor love-torn lady on Sixth Street urgently needed attention and the poor dear alcoholic gentleman on Seventh had suffered too long. Well, then, another day or two of pampering herself with all that leisure and she must get back at it.

Unaccountably, and for the first time, she began to doubt her gift. She even began to think that she might be caught. This had not occurred to her before, and because she had never told a lie in all her life, she knew that if she were ever questioned about any of the people she had helped along death's route, she would answer truthfully. So to be prepared for any emergency, however remote, that was the morning she took her light blue silk dress to the cleaners to have ready, just in case she should ever be brought to trial.

It was the last day of her holiday from her delicate craft that the bell rang. She went merrily to answer it; what she needed to put her in the mood for getting back to work was diversion.

A man was standing just outside her door when she opened it. She greeted him and he gave his name, but she was so poor when it came to names she did not notice what he said. A thought slightly strange and unsettling, but on the whole stimulating, rushed through her mind: I know this man quite well. And at the same moment, she realized that she had never seen him before. He was quite nice, a person in either late youth or very early middle age with a re- laxed, assured air. He complimented her on her geraniums and primroses and asked if he might talk with her. At her invitation he settled himself on the sofa, then he said:

"Miss Beard, I want to talk with you about crime. Are you interested in it?"

It was another survey, she thought. People were eternally making surveys on every subject and object; only the week before, she had answered a long list of questions about soaps, washing powders, and detergents.

"I don't quite know what you mean," she said and smiled. "If you're asking whether I like to read about crime, I can't say that I do. I've never been a detective- novel fan, not even when my eyes were good. I don't read about crimes in the paper either, except maybe the head- lines."

He gave a small, polite nod to acknowledge her answer. "I meant to be more specific than that," he said. "I meant to ask you if you were aware of the sharp increase in crime in this immediate neighborhood—a radius of five blocks. It's phenomenal—the increase in accidental deaths and so-called suicides. Have you noticed?"

She did not answer. She could not lie, falsehood outraged her principles. She would give the man an answer soon, but not just then; and he rushed in to fill the conversational lag, as if he were the host and she the guest to be put at ease.

"Well, I'm interested in crime," he said. "My whole family is. It started with my father. Before his death my father was a criminal psychologist. He had what some authorities called a 'genius for probing the criminal mind'—particularly murderers. He went off the deep end just once. My father knew dozens of murderers, but he said the only mass murderer he ever saw in his life he recognized when he was a child—she was a little girl in his class at school. Do you know he made very discreet investigations of that little girl throughout her adult life, and all the poor lady ever did was build up a fine record as a stenographer? Until the day my father died ten years ago, I kept twitting him about her. I told him Lombroso or anything resembling his theories was for the birds, that no one could possibly discover a murderer just by looking at her. He still insisted that respectable lady was a mass murderer. He went to his grave believing it. And he wouldn't tell me her name; he said it would make headlines some day. Aside from that one instance, my father was right on every criminal he ever dealt with—but he really was off the beam about that little girl. It was the only time anyone ever caught him out. Now, you see Miss Beard—"

And just for a moment she did not pay any attention. Now she knew the little boy's name. Now she knew why the man in front of her looked so familiar. For months she had tried to remember a name and in that instant she knew it as well as she knew her own. The little boy's name was Bobby. Bobby Williams. And this man, his son, had said that he was Lieutenant Williams. Yes, that was the name he had given when he entered her apartment.

She began to listen again.

"Miss Beard, in the Police Department we can't intuit anything. My father wouldn't be of much help in making inferences for us. We have to have proof. So when there's a marked rise in the rate of suicides and accidental deaths, we have to know why, and when those deaths occur within a small area and when most of them happen in the daytime in a neighborhood where nine-tenths of the people are away from home all day working, we still may have a tedious job, but it's something we can handle. So we start looking for someone who doesn't work, and one day one of our men notices a pleasant elderly lady who always wears white gloves and who is conveniently near after a suicide is reported, and then when we're almost positive it's she, why her suspicions are aroused and she doesn't go out any more on her little errands and for two weeks there aren't any suicides or accidental deaths. So that makes us sure she's the one. Do you see how it is?"

She did not mean to justify herself; she had no need to justify what she had done, but he was waiting for her to say something. "But don't you see," she said. "Those people were miserable. They had to die. They would have killed themselves if I hadn't done it for them."

He glared at her; it was the only time he showed any temper. "Miss Beard, people in this world have the right to their unhappiness." He was so angry he repeated himself: "Miss Beard, people in this world have the right to their unhappiness just as they have the right to their happiness. You can't go around killing people just because they're unhappy."

They talked on for awhile, and once during the rest of their conversation she thought of her blue dress and was glad that it was cleaned and ready; it was a good thing that she had been foresighted enough to think of it. And then she thought of the love-torn lady on Sixth Street and of the alcoholic gentleman on Seventh whom she had not disposed of. Poor darlings, they would just have to manage the best they could.

Then Lieutenant Williams offered her his arm, and Miss Beard, the gentle Miss Bluebeard, who had done everything quietly her whole life long, went quietly with him.

The Guy That Laughs Last
Philip Tremont

BY THE TIME HE WAS SIXTY, Big Freddy was the most powerful criminal in America and a happy man. He had reached the top not only in his chosen profession, but also in an equally demanding avocation—the production of elaborate practical jokes. He felt fairly certain of achieving his last remaining jokes. He felt fairly certain of achieving his last remaining major ambition, which was to die in bed of old age. Thus, he was not in the least alarmed when the tall brunette lovely in the Club 22 turned out to be another brakeman's daughter.

"Who's the girl over there the boys are talking to?" he now asked Dino Clark, his vice-president in charge of off-track betting.

Dino turned to study the girl in the blue jersey sheath. "I've met her, I think. Margo Something-or-other."

And then she was waving a pert good-bye to Bill Vitale, vice-president for the numbers racket, and Vinny Gio, unions, and the boys were coming over to Freddy's table.

"Who's your friend?" Freddy asked.

"Oh, Margo?" Bill said. "Just a girl. Funny thing the boss should ask about her, eh, Vinny?"

"Margo?" Vinny said. "Yeah, *she* was asking about *you*, boss. She thinks you're the handsomest guy in the room."

Freddy flushed pleasurably. He sat up straighter to slim the bulge of his waistline and patted his thinning gray hair. "Well, boys, I could believe that twenty years ago—"

"She always liked mature men," Dino said. "Told me so."

"Some broads are like that," Bill said.

"Lots of them," Vinny said.

Freddy slipped into a Mohammedan reverie. By the time he had finished half his *bouillabaisse,* he had to know more about the girl. "She married?" he asked the table at large.

"Who?" Bill asked.

"You mean Margo?" Dino asked.

"Margo's divorced," Vinny said.

"Yeah, she lives with her father," Bill said.

Freddy puckered his lips and drummed his fingers thoughtfully. A forty-year climb up from the ranks had taught him that gangsters of prominence are more often slain by ambitious underlings than by their rivals. He had learned, too, that boss hoodlums with a despotic attitude toward the girl friends of their lieutenants tended to die younger than others. That was why he wanted time to phrase his next question, for he was frequently certain that these men would cheerfully murder him, and that the only consideration staying their hands was a three-cornered distrust of each other.

For the past decade, Freddy had been gradually relinquishing his power, delegating more and more authority to the men lunching with him now. It was a deliberate program to slip into the role of elder statesman, one above the lethal rivalries of lesser chieftains. With admirable self-discipline, he had curbed his most rankling idiosyncrasies—an interest in beauty, providing it be feminine, and a fondness for staging complicated jokes. About the only fun he had out of life anymore was sending a case of spaghetti every Christmas to Lucky Luciano in exile in Italy.

But this Margo had gotten under his skin. He wanted only to be sure there was no violence-prone individual lurking in the background. "Is she anybody's girl?" he asked.

"No," Vinny said. "She's playing the field."

"She could make some guy very happy," Dino said.

"I wonder why no one has grabbed her off before now," Bill mused aloud.

"Her father is very strict," Vinny said.

A light began to dawn for Freddy. The responses were coming far too casually, with a tone that rang of rehearsal.

He stuck his fork into a *baba au rhum*. "What does her father do for a living?" he asked.

"He's a brakeman on the Long Island Railroad," Dino said.

Freddy almost choked on the pastry. He felt a sudden warm affection for Dino, Bill and Vinny, though only a moment ago he had regarded them as potential assassins. He felt like a father seeing his son graduate with honors. And his boys had spent their lifetime in a milieu which valued crude visual humor over the spoken jest. Freddy therefore took it as a compliment that they should go to such pains to set him up for the hoax he saw so plainly now. He was inordinately pleased.

The plot they had chosen was so familiar to practical jokesters that it was known under the generic term of The Engineer's Daughter. The only setting required was an isolated house in the country near a railroad track. The actors needed were a beautiful young girl and a truculent-appearing man willing to don coveralls and a railroader's cap and carry a huge pistol loaded with blanks.

The conspirators had only to convince their victim that the girl was terribly interested in him. Then, when they brought word that the fiercely possessive engineer (or fireman, or brakeman) was making an overnight run, the flattered Lothario was driven out to the waiting daughter. After the girl had enough time to say "Hi," her "father" crashed into the house, bellowing, "So you're the swine who's ruining my daughter!" and blazing away with his horse pistol. In mortal terror, the victim plunged through a window and spent the night shivering in a cornfield.

Freddy shook his head, amazed that the boys thought they could trap him with that hoary old gag—he, Big Freddy, famed for decades as the underworld's leading prankster, celebrated for the inventive comic flair he brought to even routine eliminations.

Freddy smiled inwardly, remembering . . .

There had been Big Al, for instance, boss of Chicago, where Freddy had first come into prominence. He had lured away a particularly lush chorus girl with whom

Freddy had been dallying for years by the low maneuver of proposing marriage.

Freddy was a good sport about it. He sent a handsome gift to the happy couple, danced at their wedding, and slapped the bridegroom on the back as he climbed into his touring car to begin the honeymoon trip. Bride and groom expired four miles out of town where Big Al unaccountably drove the car through a fence and off a cliff.

When their bodies were found in the morning, it was noticed that the white line dividing the highway had been painted black for some distance. A new white strip had been painted in a gentle curve that led off the road. On the shoulder of the road—beside the gap in the fence—stood a handsomely-lettered new sign: Lovers' Leap.

Then there was Big Joe, who was Freddy's predecessor as boss of the whole country. A champion swimmer in his youth, Big Joe still believed in plenty of fresh air and exercise—for everybody. He held week-long conferences and get-togethers at his country estate. An inescapable part of the regimen was a plunge into the outdoor pool at the crack of dawn, no matter what the weather or the season.

Big Joe would beat his barrel chest and bellow at his blue-lipped guests: "Swimming is the greatest conditioner in the world! Look at me! I can swim like a fish! I never miss my morning swim, summer or winter!"

The morning after Freddy's last stay at the estate (it was October), Big Joe bounced out of bed, climbed into his trunks and trotted down to the pool, his ardor for the rigorous life only slightly dimmed by the absence of anyone to herd into the freezing waters ahead of him. In the gray light of dawn, he dove happily into the pool and found himself sharing it with two angry, and hungry, tiger sharks.

Freddy was nursing a head cold when they brought him the news. "He could swim like a fish, all right," he chortled, in between sniffles, "but not as good as some of them!"

Freddy downed the last of his brandy and shook off his nostalgia. He gazed fondly at the three men sitting with him. *So they wanted to joust with the old master, did they? Well, why not have some fun with them? It would be like the old days.*

"I'd like to see that girl again," he announced.

"Who?" Dino asked.

"Margo," Vinny said. "The boss means Margo."

"Well, if you'd like to get together with her, boss," Bill said delicately, "we could probably arrange it."

"It'll be tough, though," Dino said.

"Why?" Vinny asked. "She's got big eyes for the boss. She told us so, herself."

"It's that father of hers," Bill explained. "He watches her night and day. She told us he packs a gun."

"Wait a minute," Freddy said, feeding them the next line, "didn't somebody say her father works for the railroad?"

"Yeah, that's right," they chorused blankly.

"Well," Freddy said, spreading his hands, "don't these railroad guys have to make overnight trips every couple of days?"

The word came from Dino two days later: Margo's father would be away all that night; the brakeman's daughter was even now ecstatically awaiting Freddy's coming at her father's remote Long Island home.

When Freddy stepped into Dino's Cadillac at the curb outside his Sutton Place townhouse, he found Bill and Vinny waiting in the back seat. He chuckled happily and slapped his knees as he settled between them.

Vinny passed out the cigars. Freddy accepted a light and leaned back to enjoy the long ride out to the Island, squirming to settle himself comfortably because the shoulder-holstered Luger was bulky under his arm. It was the first time he'd carried a gun in more than thirty years, he reflected. *By gosh, it was like old times.*

An hour later, Dino braked the car to a stop before a sagging two-story frame house in the wilds of Nassau County. Freddy glanced around him and grinned. The boys had chosen the site well. There was no other house in sight. The only sounds were of crickets, terribly industrious ones. And fifty yards away, he could make out the hump of the Long Island Railroad right-of-way.

"This is it," Dino said.

"Enjoy yourself, boss," Bill said, swinging open the door.

"We'll pick you up in the morning," Vinny said, slapping his back.

Freddy waved to them from the sidewalk, wondering how far away they would park. Surely close enough to see him sprint out the back door, coattails flying. When he turned back to the house, Margo stood in the open door, the lamplight behind her.

She flew into his arms when he mounted the porch. "Oh, darling, I've waited so long for this moment!"

Freddy patted her back affectionately, moving inside. "You're sure your father won't be home tonight, lovely? They tell me he carries a gun."

Her hands on his chest, Margo eased him down on the sofa. "He won't be back. Tonight is ours!"

Freddy's glance took in the scotch set out with ice and glasses on the coffee table. "Well, just in case he surprises us," he said, slipping the Luger out of the holster, "I'll be ready for him."

Margo's eyes widened in surprise and terror. "Say! What is this! They didn't tell me you'd—"

Freddy eyed her sternly. "If anybody comes through that door tonight, honey, I'll shoot this thing and shoot it straight." Carefully, he set the Luger down on his knee.

He dropped his arm around Margo's shoulders, pulling her close to him, enjoying her fright. The girl had thought she was playing a part in a harmless charade; now she was sure she was about to witness a killing.

"What are you going to do?" she wailed.

"I'm going to get the last laugh," Freddy chuckled. "I always do." He was thinking now of the poor jerk who would burst into the room in a moment, shooting off his blanks. Freddy dissolved in laughter, imagining the look on his face when he found himself staring into the Luger.

"You never heard of Lovers' Leap?" he asked the girl. Tears were streaming down his face as he tried to suck in a breath between the bursts of laughter. "You never heard of the guy who could swim like a fish?"

Margo's nails dug into his arm beseechingly. "Please! Get out of here!"

The front door slammed. "Margo!" a voice bellowed. "Who have you got in here with you?"

"No one!" the girl shrieked. "No one! Absolutely no one!"

"It's too late now," Freddy said, holding the Luger out, leveling it.

"So you're the fiend who's ruining my daughter!" There, like an old-time actor, stood the brakeman, in coveralls and a long-peaked cap that shaded his eyes, the spout on his oil can fully two feet long, a huge cartridge belt cinched around his waist. The muzzle of the ancient revolver in his hand looked as large as the entrance to the Holland Tunnel.

"Stand up and get your head blown off like a man," the brakeman intoned. A thick woolly mustache was glued under his nose. He raised the revolver until it was aimed dead center at Freddy's forehead. Flame and noise belched from the gun.

Freddy brought the Luger from behind his back.

"Run, honey!" Margo screamed.

Freddy aimed carefully and squeezed off the whole clip.

The ludicrous oil can dropped from the brakeman's hand. The girl leaped from the sofa and threw herself into the man's arms. Unaccountably, he was still on his feet. Freddy had known the man would not slump to the floor dead—the Luger, too, was loaded with blanks—but he'd imagined that his target would flee in fright.

Two figures emerged from the shadows of the hall and stood beside the smiling brakeman. Vinny and Bill. His arm around the girl's waist, Dino raised the hand that still held the pistol and tossed off the peaked cap and plucked loose the bushy mustache. The three men wore broad smiles.

Freddy's jaw dropped. Then he grinned shamefacedly. "You sure topped me this time boys. I must be getting old." A chill knot of fear was growing in his stomach. There was a loud roaring in his ears.

Dino glanced at his watch. "That's the helicopter, right on time."

"We figured you'd figure this old gag out," Bill told Freddy."

"And we figured you'd spring a gun," Vinny said.

"Loaded with blanks, naturally. You wouldn't commit any murders at this stage of your career." He held a slim automatic in his hand, the muzzle pointing negligently at Freddy's midriff.

"The first bullet in this old cannon was a blank," Dino said.

"But the rest aren't," Bill said. He, too, held a gun.

"You see," Vinny said, "we figure we don't really need you and your corny gags now that you've given us so much power in the organization. Our problem of stepping into your shoes up to now has been that we didn't trust each other. But we worked out this way for us all to have the goods on each other."

"All we needed," Dino said, "was for your body to be found miles away from where the cops could figure we could possibly be. In a minute, a helicopter is going to land on the front lawn. Two minutes after it puts us down on the roof of a warehouse in Jersey, fifty miles from here, we'll be guests at a testimonial dinner for a retiring police chief. Sweet alibi, eh?"

Looking into the raised pistols, Freddy still couldn't believe it. "You went to an awful lot of trouble with this scheme, boys."

"We wanted to have the last laugh, for once," Dino said.

"That's right," Vinny and Bill said.

And then they pulled the triggers.

Diet and Die
Wenzell Brown

SIR, YOU APPEAR TO BE a gentleman of taste and discrimination, such a man as I believe myself to be. I am informed that you are a psychiatrist and this training should add to your insight and wisdom. I have refused to make my confession in the presence of the police. They are dull, unimaginative clods, quite incapable of understanding the sensitivities that come with refinement and breeding. Sir, I am a murderer. I admit the fact. But many fastidious men have been preoccupied with violent death. I consider it no disgrace to be a member of their ranks. Nor do I hope to escape the penalty involved. However, I see no reason to invite the mockery, the crude guffaws, perhaps the disbelief of the uncouth minions of the law who, until your arrival, were my inquisitors.

I must tell you about Yvette, but first it becomes necessary to speak a few words about myself. My lineage is one of distinction and I am naturally aware of the social prestige attached to my family name. The question therefore arises why I should have married Yvette, who was not only nine years my senior but also a woman whose rather coarse appearance indicated, with accuracy, her French peasant stock.

But I am getting ahead of my story. Of my youth, let it suffice to say that it was spent in luxurious loneliness. My father was too preoccupied with his business interests to give me more than a passing thought. My mother was a woman of artistic temperament who attempted to instill in me her love of art, music and poetry. In retrospect it seems as though my entire boyhood was spent in museums, literary salons and art galleries. Mother virtually commuted

from Boston to Europe and I invariably accompanied her.
True, there were a few brief intervals in private schools but
these interludes are filled with painful memories. Grubby
dormitories, the juvenile atrocities of the playing fields and
the public humiliation of the classroom were not for me.
Worst of all was the tasteless refectory food. Before long
I would fall ill and mother, taking pity on my misery, would
swoop down and remove me from my sordid surroundings.

By and large, my education was supervised by a series of
tutors who coached me in languages, art and music. Not
altogether successfully, I must admit. My talents are
limited. I am a connoisseur rather than a creative artist.
Nevertheless, under this irregular tutelage, I did gain an
admission to one of our better universities. I was not happy
there. The conditions that prevail at such institutions are
deplorably primitive, especially in the matter of food. I
withdrew in my sophomore year.

My mother and I resumed our travels. Although I may be
considered a failure, there was one area in which I had
become an expert. My judgment in the culinary arts was
impeccable. Wherever mother and I went, be it Paris, Rome
or Vienna, I was able to ferret out little out-of-the-way
restaurants where the cuisine was superb. Mother and her
friends always deferred to my judgment and I never led
them astray.

My father's demise passed almost unnoticed but mother's
death six years ago came as a severe blow, especially as it
was accompanied by the shocking knowledge that the
family fortune had dwindled to a point of almost non-
existence. Through a series of circumstances too elaborate
to recount, I found myself stranded in New York, saddled
with an unpleasant job that paid me a mere pittance. New
York has always seemed to me a coldly hostile city.
Certainly it was not designed for a man of my sensibilities.

I had never possessed the knack of easy friendships and
now I was quite alone. Night after night I wandered about
the city, seeking the side streets in the hope of finding cosy
little restaurants where fine foods would be served. Invariably I was disappointed. Time and again I would rush
out of restaurants in a rage, the food barely tasted. Every-

thing was wrong, the sauces abominable, the legumes over-cooked, bread and pastries either a puffy mess or hard as shoe leather.

Life was intolerable until one night I stumbled by chance on a winding side street in Greenwich Village and a wooden sign that read Chez Yvette. I wandered in without hope. The place was dark and dreary, with small tables lit only by candles thrust into the necks of Chianti bottles. The menu was in French but I had been fooled too often for this to arouse my expectations. My spirits were dampened further by the drab slattern of a waitress who took my order.

I selected fillets of sole *au gratin*. It is a simple dish which even the inexpert cook should be able to prepare tolerably well. The restaurant was almost empty, and I tapped my foot with impatience over the long delay. At length the waitress returned with a covered tray. As soon as the lid was lifted I knew that I found what I had sought for so long, a cook who was absolute mistress of her craft. The sole could not have been better. The sauce Provençale was exquisite, the forcemeat stuffing a dream. The vintage wine which accompanied the meal was perfection.

I could scarcely believe my good fortune and I demanded to be taken to the kitchen to present my compliments to the cook. Yvette was standing by the stove, her black hair straggly, her swarthy face beaded with sweat. She was an enormous woman, her shapeless figure encased in a rusty black dress, her thick legs covered with black cotton stockings. But to me she was beautiful. I kissed her on both cheeks and hugged her.

Yvette was delighted to find an appreciative customer. Soon we were talking a mile a minute, both ecstatic in our discoveries. From then on I rarely missed a night at Chez Yvette. She prepared all sorts of delicacies for me, sweetbreads *à la* Brunilesco, lobster *à la* Borgia, *galantine* of capon *à la* Persano. She would hover over me while I dined and often, after the front lights had been dimmed, she would join me over a glass of wine or black coffee served with the most delectable of French pastries.

She was a treasure and I could not let her go, but unfortunately my reserve of cash was running low. Yvette's flair for cookery did not dim the shrewd financial calculations which were an essential characteristic of her French peasant ancestry. I was well fed but I paid through the nose, and I could not afford to pay much longer. Yvette sensed my dilemma and it was she who struck the bargain. One evening after we had dined, she suggested that I stay the night. I was already in her debt and I could scarcely refuse. When the restaurant was closed, I followed her to her room above the kitchen with considerable reluctance.

We undressed in the dark and I slipped into the old-fashioned, four-poster bed beside her. My misgivings were groundless. Yvette's approach to love was direct and forthright. My previous experience with fashionably slender young women of my acquaintance seemed, by comparison, shallow, bloodless, pale carbon copies of passion.

The next week we were married. At first the marriage was a happy one. Shortly afterward I came into a small legacy which I invested in enlarging the restaurant and in advertising. Soon we were doing a thriving business. The discriminating, with a few paid plugs from columnists, found their way to our door. Yvette continued to cook. I decorated an upper room and held a sort of informal court here. The room was open only to gourmets who sought my advice in the selection of their dishes. Yvette and I planned the meals together. Often I spent the mornings scouring the markets for the necessary ingredients for the day's bill of fare.

The restaurant became the very core of my existence. It gave me dignity and stature as a man. I loved it and I loved Yvette because she was an integral part of it. I was happier than I had ever been.

Then tragedy struck without warning. Yvette had complained of aches and pains, of exhaustion at night. I advised a medical checkup but Yvette's reluctance to pay a doctor's fee restrained her from following my advice until she actually collapsed in the kitchen.

Yvette returned from the clinic gray-faced and shaken. Her excessive weight had brought on a coronary condition complicated by incipient diabetes. The doctor had prescribed a rigorous diet. Yvette had protested.

"You have no choice," he told her. "Either diet or die."

Yvette was a determined woman. Once convinced that dieting was a necessity, she approached her problem with rocklike fortitude. No longer did she sip the vichyssoise which she prepared, or slip a strawberry tart from the tray into her mouth.

Yvette's reduction in weight was phenomenal. Within a few months she was scarcely recognizable as the fat, jolly, easygoing woman I had married. Her figure became slim and solid; her face, planed down, showed a fine bold bone structure. I would not say that she was beautiful. The descriptive word "handsome" might apply better. Certainly she was striking. Deprived of her interest in food, she became impassioned with her appearance, which she had previously neglected. She was rigorously corseted, her hair coiffed with painstaking care and she became adept in the use of makeup.

My coterie of friends congratulated me on the change but soon they began to drift away from Chez Yvette. More and more my wife became indifferent to the preparation of those dishes which had given a certain fame to the restaurant. She hired a chef of mediocre talents and her supervision was limited to seeing that he prepared the day's menu with the maximum of economy.

With the change in her appearance came a complete alteration of her personality. She had always been thrifty but now she developed a mean, niggardly streak. She substituted dried mushrooms for the fresh ones required in Allemande sauce. She even mixed pig's liver in the *pâté de foie gras* and, most frightful of all, employed margarine in the preparation of vegetables. My protests were without avail. Soon she was serving smaller portions and, one by one, she eliminated the dishes requiring long preparation and expensive ingredients.

Our exclusive clientele dropped off but Yvette was not disturbed. The restaurant was being filled by a new type of customer, tourists with barbarian tastes, clerks and typists from nearby office buildings, hoi polloi from the housing development in the next block. Yvette moved from the kitchen to the cashier's desk. She made a careful survey of the neighborhood's desires and came up with a menu of salads, sandwiches and businessmen's special blue plates.

Our personal relations deteriorated rapidly. Previously she had deferred to my judgments and I had believed that she considered herself fortunate indeed in finding a husband of refined tastes and superior social position. But now I was a supernumerary. She did not trust me with the marketing but attended to all purchases herself. Our marriage was disintegrating. Her pliancy and docility disappeared. By bedtime she was usually too exhausted by the day's labor and her rigorous diet to respond to my overtures and on such occasions as she did, she tended to be harsh, demanding, and even critical of my male prowess.

Before long my affection for her changed to hate. I could not stand the sight of her bold, hawklike features. Her eyes which had seemed jolly in their casements of flesh, now had a predatory gleam. But all these shortcomings might have been tolerable were it not for the fact that the food became increasingly execrable. Yvette had developed into a fanatic in the matter of diet. Like the reformed drunkard, she sought converts with a crusader's zeal. The room which had once been reserved exclusively for myself and my friends was changed into a health bar.

It was bad enough not to be able to get a proper meal in my own home but Yvette did not stop at that. She constantly nagged at me for what she termed an excessive interest in food. She plied me with carrot juice, cottage cheese and rye crisp and, when I spurned them, made derogatory remarks concerning my expanding waistline.

My quest for gastronomic pleasure led me far afield but with only the most miniscule success until I discovered the Golden Cock and Germaine Duval. The Golden Cock was on the East Side in the upper Seventies, a shabby basement affair which one could pass a thousand times and hardly notice. But where else in the city could one secure such exquisitely prepared tomato and shrimp soup or cabbage à la petite russienne?

Germaine was even larger than Yvette when I had first known her, and, I should judge, a few years older. Her hair was peroxided an incredible yellow but her cheeks were smooth and pink, her eyes a pale blue. I will not say that it was love at first sight but there was a reciprocated attraction born of a common interest. In the realm of gastronomy, Germaine was a prima donna who craved the applause of a virtuoso to exploit her talents. As such we complemented each other perfectly. Happiness once more seemed within my reach.

Yvette, however, proved difficult. She bitterly resented my evenings out. She controlled the purse strings and drew them tight. Willy-nilly, I must be satisfied with the insipid fare of the Chez Yvette and my wife's dwindling charms. Yvette was a good Catholic and divorce was out of the question. On occasion I pilfered the cash box and spent a night with Germaine but Yvette developed a positive genius in thwarting these excursions. Without a penny in my pocket, I would be forced to take the table reserved for me in the health bar where Yvette would serve me a tomato surprise, wheat germ bread and a serving of artificially flavored gelatine.

Is it any wonder that my thoughts turned to murder? As you can readily see, I am not a man to whom violence comes naturally. I have never discharged a firearm and the thought of using a knife or the proverbial blunt instrument was enough to set my teeth on edge. Poison was the only conceivable means of ridding myself of Yvette's unwanted ministrations. I considered the possibilities. Arsenic. Cyanide. Both were too obvious. Besides, how could I secure them without leaving a trail or administer them without arousing suspicion? I brooded over my problem but could find no answers until Yvette herself provided the perfect solution.

Our bedroom had taken on much the appearance of an apothecary shop. The tops of Yvette's bureau and dresser were crammed with boxes and bottles of pills and capsules. Yvette subscribed to various papers and magazines, cutting out all articles relating to drugs used in reducing and dietary aids. A number of patrons of the restaurant were on diets and Yvette held long discussions with them, comparing the efficacy of the methods which they employed.

Among the new drugs appearing on the market was one which was sold under the trade name of Yarubex. It could not be purchased in America but was widely advertised in Mexico. One of Yvette's friends who had made a trip south of the border brought her back a bottle. The tiny pellets were white and looked completely harmless. Yvette might have dosed herself with them but, on the same day that they were given to her, *The New York Times* printed a condensation of a bulletin released by the United States Department of Health. The article issued a sharp warning against Yarubex. The little pellets could be lethal when taken in excessive quantities. Diabetics were in particular danger. A score of deaths had already been reported.

Yvette sputtered and fumed over her narrow escape. However her ingrained parsimony forbade her to dispose of the pills. Instead, she thrust them in the back of the medicine closet, where I discovered them a few days later. I examined them with interest. They were almost exact replicas of the saccharin tablets which Yvette used daily. I poured out a few of them and mixed them in with the saccharin already in Yvette's gold-encrusted miniature pillbox. The substitution was made almost automatically, without any real hope or any feeling of guilt. I could not believe that my problem would be solved with such ease.

Two days later Yvette was dead. I came home in the afternoon and found her sprawled across the bed, fully clothed. I made certain of her death by checking her pulse and heart beat, then I went through her purse for the pillbox. I dumped its contents into the toilet and refilled it with saccharin. I removed the bottle of Yarubex from the medicine cabinet and placed it on her bedside table. Then I called the police.

A Lieutenant Stevens was in charge of the investigation that followed. He is a bluff, crude man and at first he appeared mildly suspicious. But there was not and could not be any proof of malfeasance on my part. Soon the matter was dropped and Yvette was listed officially as another victim of unscrupulous racketeers in the drug business.

The next few months were very busy ones. I sold Chez Yvette at a handsome profit. My evenings were spent at the Golden Cock. I looked up some of my old cronies and soon the word was spread that meals to fit the tastes of an epicure were available again. As soon as a reasonable time had elapsed, Germaine and I were married. Life reassumed the same happy glow of the early days of my marriage with Yvette. I was a contented man.

I should have known it was too good to last. One day Germaine came to me with tears in her eyes. "Darling," she cried, "the doctor says I have to go on a diet."

Sir, you are a man of imagination. I will not bore you with repetitious details. It would be like the rerun of a film or watching a play for the second time, with only minor variations. Germaine and Yvette were so much alike in their reactions. And then, of course, I met Suzanne. I realize it was incredibly stupid of me to use the same murder method twice. I can only excuse myself on the basis that the temptation to repeat a perfect crime is almost compulsive. Besides how could I foresee that Lieutenant Stevens would have been transferred from Greenwich Village to the district in which I was now living?

However, I comfort myself that in the annals of crime my case will remain unique. I should imagine that many a murderer has killed his victim for the price of a square meal. But is there another instance of a man who has risked the death penalty twice to secure dishes that are exquisitely prepared, superbly served?

At least I can look forward to one more such dinner. Does not the condemned man have the privilege of selecting his final meal? There is a dish which is described by Alexandre Dumas which I have never tried. Hare chops à la Melville. But perhaps that is expecting too much of prison cuisine. Something more simple must do. A Kirsch omelet, I should think. Preparation is not difficult. I can supply the recipe myself. Six eggs, a pinch of salt, three tablespoons of sugar—

Ah, but I can see your interest is lagging. Quite correctly so. These details can be discussed later.

Just for Kicks
Richard Marsten

IT WAS SAD about Charlie Franklin.

The saddest part, of course, was his apparent happiness. To look at him, you'd never guess he was filled with anything but wild, soaring joy. He was, after all, a handsome man of thirty-four years, and a bachelor to boot. As art director of Smith, Carruthers, Cole and Carney—a Madison Avenue advertising agency—his salary, by the most conservative estimate, probably fell somewhere between forty and fifty thousand dollars a year, not to mention Christmas bonuses and all the models he could date. He had dated quite a few of them. Invariably they'd come to see his apartment after an evening of fun and revelry. He lived in the top two floors of a discreet brownstone on Seventieth Street, just off Park Avenue. The walls of his duplex were covered with many high-quality prints and several originals, including a pencil drawing which Picasso had made on a tablecloth and which had cost Charlie two thousand dollars the summer he was getting drunk on La Costa Brava. Since he still got drunk occasionally, his liquor cabinet was stocked with expensive whiskeys. His closets were packed with hand-tailored clothes. His kitchen shelves brimmed with fine China and rare gourmet treats.

But Charlie Franklin was a very sad man.

He tried to explain this to Ed Bell, the firm's copy chief, one midnight in the dead of January. The men had been working late on a particularly tough nut, a presentation for the Fabglo Lipstick account. It must be said here that Smith, Carruthers, Cole and Carney was a very high-type advertising agency which had been known to drop backward accounts who were not forward-thinking. Its advertising consisted mainly of striking photographic layouts coupled with terse provocative copy, usually of the one-line-sell variety. Once, a world-famous airline refused to believe that the agency could explain radar-guided flight in a single line of copy. Well, Smith, Carruthers, Cole and Carney promptly showed those backward-thinking cotton-pickers the door. That was the way they worked. Proud, you might say.

The men had been in the office all that night trying to conjure up a striking photographic layout which they could then couple with their characteristically provocative hunk of one-line copy. They had finally vanquished the elusive beast. The photograph would show a statuesque blonde wearing nothing but Fabglo Lipstick. In concession to *The New York Times* and its genteel advertising department, the girl would be carrying a primitive war club, strategically and concealingly draped across her prow. At the maiden's feet would be a disorderly pile of unconscious cavemen. The copy would read "KNOCK THEM DEAD WITH FABGLO RED." The ad was a thing to stir imaginations and cause the heart to beat faster. It would also, they hoped, sell lipstick. So the men clapped each other on the back and went to Charlie's pad for an overdue nightcap. They couldn't go to Ed Bell's pad because Ed was a commuter who lived fifty miles away in a ten-room colonial which you might not want to call a "pad" to begin with. So they went to Charlie's duplex.

It was while Charlie was pouring out liberal doses of Canadian Club that he said, "Are you pleased with it, Ed?"

Ed Bell was by nature a very cautious and nervous man, the type who starts at every sound. His enthusiasm that night, however, knew no bounds. "The ad, do you mean?" he said. "Charlie, I think we've got a skyrocket here. Let's just hope Fabglo doesn't throw water on the fuse before we get it on the launching platform."

"But does it please you?" Charlie asked.

"It gasses me," Ed said. "It's stimulating and thought-provoking. It's artistic and sophisticated." He paused. "It's also somewhat sexy. Why? Something bother you about it?"

"Well, I . . ."

"What's the matter, Charlie?"

"I don't know what it is, Ed. But . . . Well, I just don't seem to get a charge out of things."

Ed thought this over for a moment. "You've thrown out your line and got a nibble," he said. "Now bring the tuna aboard."

"I don't know how to put it more plainly, Ed. I just don't get a bang out of things."

"You mean your work? The agency?"

"No. I mean everything."

"Everything? Well now, you've started a landslide. So let's dig some of the rocks away and try to find daylight. How long have you felt this way? You can confide in me."

"All my life," Charlie said.

"You mean . . . nothing's ever given you a charge? Nothing?"

"Nothing," Charlie said glumly.

"Girls?"

"Not even girls," Charlie said. "No matter what their size, shape, and frame of mind."

"Well now, Charlie," Ed said cautiously, "you've just dropped an H-bomb. Let's come out of the shelter and check our Geigers. Maybe the fallout isn't as bad as the blast. You don't like women, so okay. Any man can get around to feeling like so. But there are other things in life, Charlie."

"Like for instance?"

"Like for instance," and here Ed held up his glass, "booze."

"I've tasted every liquor, wine, cordial, and beer on the market. Domestic, imported, and bathtub. I've had it straight, mixed, and in coffee, tea, and even milk. I've thrown a jigger of rye and a jigger of scotch into the same glass of beer and then drank it. I mixed rum, gin, and bourbon in the blender with a slice of lime. I've even drunk hair tonic. No kicks, Ed. No bang."

"There are stronger things than whiskey," Ed said, his

voice dropping to a conspiratorial whisper. He looked at Charlie expectantly. Charlie shook his head.

"I've tried marijuana, cocaine, heroin, morphine, dolophon, opium, and any drug you'd care to name. I've mixed heroin and cocaine in what is called a 'speedball.' I've smoked it, sniffed it, skin-popped it, and mainlined it. Once I soaked a stick of marijuana in a martini, dried it off, and then smoked it." He paused. Sadly, he said, "No bang."

"Mmmm,"Ed said. "Well, let's take a walk in the woods and see if there's anything in the traps we set. How about music? Surely music pleases you."

"I began with the three B's," Charlie said, "same place everyone starts. Then I moved to the Russians. Tschaikovsky, Rimsky-Korsakov, Borodin, Mussourgsky, Balakirev, and Cui. No kicks. I tried Chabrier, Stravinsky, Hanson, Holst and Ravel. No charge. I mowed through every classical composer living or dead or aging or sick."

"What about popular stuff?"

"I went from jazz to swing to cool bop to hard bop to rock and roll. I've run the gamut from Bix Beiderbecke through Thelonius Monk to Sal Mineo. I've even bought chilren's records, for God's sake. Have you ever heard Tubby the Tuba?"

"No," Ed admitted.

"No bang," Charlie said, "I've even listened to madrigals and Gregorian chants. Folk music. Voodoo mumbo-jumbo."

"No bang?" Ed said.

"No bang."

"Well, how about art, man? That's your first love. Doesn't *that* excite you?"

"I've seen everything from the cave drawings up. I sure don't understand all of it—but I don't like any of it."

"Not even your Picasso tablecloth?" Ed asked astonished.

"Not even that. I'm thinking of taking it down and sending it to the laundry."

"Well now, don't get nervous," Ed said nervously. "There are other things in life. Let's just send up a few trial rockets and see if we can leave a stain on the Moon, okay? You've got theatres and . . ."

"Who wants to see sick plays about queer people and spinsters in Venice?"

". . . and movies . . ."

"Who wants travelogues in Cinemascope?"

". . . and books! Charlie, there are millions of books!"

"I'm reading now," Charlie said glumly. "It's my latest project, but it won't be any different, I know it. I started with *Beowulf,* and it was putrid. I've been working my way up through the centuries. Shakespeare was corny and Hemingway was trite. I'm reading the bestseller list stuff now, but I'm bored to tears. It's no use, Ed. There's just nothing in life that gives me any kicks. I even hated baseball and ice cream when I was a kid." He looked for a moment as if he would cry. "Aw, what's the use?" he asked plaintively. "Food is bland, and nature is dull. Men are uninteresting, and women are unexciting. I've seen it all and heard it all and tasted it all and felt it all, and it all stinks. There's nothing left."

"Well," Ed said morosely, "I wish I could help you, Charlie."

"You can't."

"Maybe I ought to run along home. Maybe you need sleep."

"What's the sense in sleeping?" Charlie said. "You only have to get up in the morning."

Ed put on his coat. "Don't let this throw you," he advised. "Look around for a hold, and then pin this to the mat."

Charlie smiled. "Sure," he said.

At the door, Ed shook hands with him and then paused, listening. "What's that?" he said.

Charlie listened, too. "Somebody getting home downstairs," he said.

"Man, how can you stand living in the city?" Ed said. "Aren't you afraid of burglars?"

"A burglar might be interesting."

Ed patted his arm. "Look, get some sleep, will you?" he said.

"There's a book I want to finish first."

Hopefully, Ed said, "Oh? Something interesting?"

"So-so."

"What's the title?"

"Compulsion," Charlie said.

It would be unfair to say that this novel about two boys who commit a thrill murder first gave Charlie the idea of killing just for kicks. The book strongly condemned the act of the would-be supermen, and Charlie was hardly an impressionable juvenile-delinquent type. But in much the same way as the boys' minds were infatuated with the printed words of Nietzsche, so too was Charlie lured by *these* printed words.

In the studio the next day, posing a model for a perfume ad which read, "THE SWEET SMELL OF DANGER: EAU DE BOUQUET," Charlie obviously did not have his mind on his work. The model was an overflowing brunette clad in a pale diaphanous wrapper and clutching, for effect, a bunch of flowers. Oddly, people from every department in the agency kept dropping in on Charlie while he posed the girl. Oddly, all of the visitors were men, but they nonetheless had very pertinent questions to ask of the art director.

One fellow asked, "Should I use a 1-H or a 2-H pencil for these rough sketches, Charlie?"

Another asked, "How do you spell 'cat,' Charlie?"

An office boy entered agog and asked, "Is it all right to empty the wastebasket in your office, Mr. Franklin?"

Charlie seemed very tolerant of the interruptions. The brunette model, slightly chilled in the sheer wrapper, kept clutching the flowers for effect.

"Bend over a little, please," Charlie said, and the girl did so with amazingly abundant alacrity. The photographer, unwilling to believe the beauty he had seen inverted in the ends of his camera, pulled his head from beneath the black hood and blinked his eyes.

"That's nice," Charlie said. "Now hold it."

Charlie was thinking it might not be a bad idea to kill somebody, just to see if there'd be a thrill in it. The one thing, in fact, which didn't send him into the street in instant search of a victim was the possibility that even a murder might not provide any kicks. And what could he do then? Ride a Mongolian pony? Join the Russian Air Force? Climb a flagpole in Topeka? If this ultimate experience of taking another man's life failed to give him a bang, what on earth could he try next?

Where's your gumption, Charlie Franklin? he asked himself.

Be American, for God's sake! How will you know whether or not the thrill is there until you try it? Did you know, for example, that oysters with oatmeal provided no charge until you'd tried that delicate dish? Of course not! Did you know that Shostakovitch played backwards was as uninspiring as and far more cacaphonous than Shostakovitch played forwards—until you'd tried it? How can you tell if there's going to be any fun in anything until you try it? Where's your native initiative? Where's your spark, Charlie boy?

You're right, he told himself silently. Aloud to the model, he said, "Dear, close the wrapper a little. You'll catch cold." But he didn't even look at her.

His mind was made up. He would kill somebody, just for kicks. If it worked out, fine. If not, so it didn't matter.

So he laid his plans.

If there was to be a killing, it would have to be a perfect one. Charlie was far too sensitive a man to even think of allowing himself to fall into the hands of the police. His victim, therefore, could not be his mother, although he admitted with wry psychiatric chucklings that she was his first choice. Nor could he pick a victim at random as the boys in the book had done. There were too many imponderables in such a plan of action. If there was some danger in choosing a victim whose personal habits were well-known, there was a converse safety factor in knowing the chosen victim would perform in a way which could be predetermined.

Fondly, with loving care, he chose Ed Bell as the victim.

Ed was a bachelor who, like Charlie, lived alone. Unlike Charlie, Ed was a highly nervous man who had been un-

able to endure the uncertain and frightening clutter of
New York City. Ed had voluntarily become a commuter
who lived in northern Westchester on a six-acre tract of
land upon which stood his old colonial house. Ed chose a
colonial because he wanted to hear the rich squeak of old
burnished timbers under his feet. He wanted to see antique
exposed beams in the ceiling. Besides, an old house was
cheaper than building a new one. He had named his place
Bell's Toll, the title being an inverted pun, ha, on the price
he paid daily in the city in order to enjoy his creaky re-
treat in the exurbs. But whatever price he was forced to
pay in the rat race, Ed Bell had surely achieved aloneness.

His nearest crotchety neighbor, two acres away, was
shielded from him by a magnificent stand of pines—"These
stately American monarchs," the real estate agent had
said—the very presence of which had increased the price
of the acreage by several thousand dollars. The pines,
monarchs that they were, provided a very formidable
sight and sound barrier against the crotchety modern house
on the right of Ed's colonial. To the left of Ed's house were
four choice acres of his own land, twelve acres of un-
developed land which was used as a garbage dumping
area for the town, and then a factory which made Christmas
balls. The factory was owned by the Town Supervisor,
which, Ed perhaps unjustly felt, accounted for its presence
in a residential-zoned area. In any case, Ed knew complete
solitude at night. Screened from the modern monstrosity,
separated from the penetratingly sweet aroma of burning
garbage by his own four acres, a long way away from the
Christmas-ball makers, Ed felt like an island indeed. The
country was essential to his peace of mind. He'd actually
been frightened all the while he lived in New York. Lying
alone in his narrow bed, he would listen to the sounds of
traffic, starting at every backfire, listening to footsteps in
the hallway of his apartment building, frightful lest some
burglar or some drunken individual stumble into his apartment. In a highly pressurized business like Ed's, where a
single line of copy spoke volumes, it was no wonder he
was a nervous man.

But the country, Charlie assumed, had demolished all of

Ed's fears and anxieties. Ed went to bed every night at ten o'clock—except on weekends, of course. On weekends, oh that gay dog went to local dramatic productions and church socials and all sorts of wild and gay revelries in northern Westchester. But during the week, he avoided all temptation. He would arrive in town at 7:16, drive from the station to his house in a Volkswagen, prepare his own dinner, read awhile, lock the doors and windows—a dreadful habit left over from his cautious, nervous city existence—and then go to sleep. By six the next morning, he would be ready to enter the rat race again, a rested and contented man.

Charlie planned to kill him while he slept. That was the only humane thing to do, and Charlie did not wish to be cruel to an old friend. He also knew exactly which weapon he would use, the only logical and practical weapon, it seemed to him: a crossbow.

He probably would have made his murder attempt sooner, but he had a little difficulty turning up a crossbow. He finally found one in a Third Avenue antique shop. When the proprietor asked him, "Going to hang it over the fireplace?" Charlie answered, "No, going to kill someone with it."

The proprietor laughed all over the place. "Better give you the arrows then, huh?" he said, holding his sides.

"One arrow will be enough," Charlie said, for that was all he planned to use. He had not shot spitballs from a rubberband with deadly accuracy as a boy for nothing.

So, carefully, he laid his plans. Unfortunately, the planning brought him no joy. Hopefully, he prayed the actual murder would.

On a Wednesday in February, as Ed was leaving the office at five, Charlie approached him. "Are you going straight home tonight?" he asked.

"Yes," Ed said. "Why?"

"Thought you might stop at my place for a drink," Charlie said, not meaning the invitation at all, of course.

"Thanks, some other time, Charlie," Ed said. "I want to eat and hit the sack. I'm bushed."

"You'll probably have people dropping in all night long," Charlie said with probing shrewdness.

"No, I don't socialize during the week," Ed affirmed. "You know that. I'll be in bed by eight-thirty. I don't like February anyway. It depresses me. I'd rather be in bed than sitting around. February's a rotten month, don't you think?"

"How do you mean?"

"I don't know. Spooky. Eerie. Sounds outside the house, wind blowing, brrrrr, makes me nervous." He shuddered a little. "How's your problem coming, Charlie?"

"I'm working on it," Charlie said.

"Good. Lead it to the scaffold, and I'll hold the basket," Ed said.

"I'll try. Good night, Ed. Sleep tight."

"You said it," Ed said, and he left the office.

At eight o'clock that night, the crossbow on the front seat of the car, Charlie started the drive to northern Westchester. He hoped to be there by nine-thirty at the latest, at which time he would shoot an arrow into Ed Bell's heart. The police, in their wisdom, would conclude, after much thought, that an Indian had killed Ed. And while they combed the country's reservations, Charlie would sit back and enjoy—he hoped—the pleasure of what he'd done.

He reached Bell's Toll at nine-thirty. He parked the car near the stand of American monarchs, doused the lights, and then started up the driveway on foot. There was the smell of growing Westchester things in the air, and the smell of burning Westchester garbage. Carrying the crossbow, Charlie sniffed deeply of the air. He did not walk on the gravel. He walked soundlessly instead on the soft turf at the side of the drive. The big colonial house came into view. Not a light was burning. Ed, then, was already asleep. Charlie listened to the sound of the wind, and the sound of the shutters banging against the clapboard of the house. He had felt no joy of anticipation on the ride up, and he felt no joy now, no excitement. He wondered again if the murderer would provide the thrill he was seeking. He refused to believe otherwise. There simply *had* to be some good things in life. At nine forty-five, using a chisel, he forced the front door.

He was familiar with the house, having been Ed's legitimate guest there on many occasions. His eyes, too, were already accustomed to the darkness. He moved swiftly toward the staircase leading to the bedrooms upstairs. He was not at all nervous. When the old burnished timbers squeaked richly under his feet, he paid them no mind. The door to the master bedroom was just ahead at the end of the hall. Charlie cocked the crossbow and walked toward it. He listened for a moment, and then eased the door open. He still felt no thrill of anticipation. Doubt again crossed his mind. *Would* this provide the charge, the kicks, the bang? The door creaked noisily on its Revolutionary War hinges. There was a moment's stillness, and then Ed sat upright in bed. Trained by years of interrupted city sleep, fearful of the February night noises, he stared into the darkness and his voice crackled briskly across the length of the room.

"Who is it!"

Charlie did not answer. He raised the crossbow and leveled it at the bed. Ed moved with amazing swiftness. There was a medley of sound in the next instant, Ed's shout, and then the noise of a drawer sliding open swiftly, and then another louder shocking noise.

And Charlie Franklin, for the first and last time, finally got a real bang out of life.

He got it when Ed yanked the pistol from the night-table drawer and shot him twice in the head.

Please Forgive Me
Henry Kane

HIDDEN SUN TINCTURED SULLEN CLOUDS with a burning tint of orange. There was no wind and it was hot, steaming-hot; summer heat clung to the streets like sweat. It had rained all night, but it was massing now for rain again, or fog.

Paul Matthew, in his bedroom, sighed as he dropped the slat of the venetian blind. He went away from the window, padded to the bathroom for a cold shower; then he shaved, pulled on slacks, loafers and a sport shirt. He ambled to a tall chest, slid open a drawer, drew out a revolver and a belt-holster. He broke the revolver, carefully examined the fully loaded cylinder, straightened the gun, slipped it into the holster, buckled that to his belt. He sighed again as he opened a closet, reached in for a jacket.

Hot, he thought, *for a jacket, but you just can't walk around with a gun sticking out of you like it's a flower you wear in your lapel.*

He shrugged into the jacket, winced as a sudden cascade of rock and roll music burst from the lower floor. There was handclapping to the beat, a female giggle and male laughter. He crossed to the bedroom door, shut it, turned for a glance at the mirror.

Look like a vacation-time young guy going out to the ball game, he thought. *Except for the gray hair at the temples. No kick about the figure either—tall enough, straight enough, only a hint of belly.* Fine, everything would be fine, except for the worry written around his eyes. He did not want that to show. Worry was not for wearing on the outside. Worry should be hidden, like the gun. He began a sigh again, smothered it, fixed a smile on his face and went down to breakfast.

The rock and roll was coming from the living room; he

looked in. Billy was dancing with the girl, Kate—flinging her about in a knee-bumping dance; Sal Richmond, body bent, wriggling, was clapping his hands and tapping his feet, his dark eyes glistening as he watched the dance. They were so much alike, the two boys, tall and thin and black-haired, except that Billy's eyes were blue. The girl seemed older than either of them, more mature, her hips wrapped in tight blue jeans, her red-checked blouse open deep. Sal saw him first and stopped the clapping; then the dance ended and Billy grinned sheepishly.

"Good morning, Dad," Billy said.

"It's afternoon," Paul Matthew said.

"Morning for you, though," Billy said.

"Yes, morning for me," Paul Matthew said testily. "Good morning, everybody."

"Could you stand some more music?" the girl inquired, at the record player.

"Please, I'd rather you didn't," Paul Matthew said.

"You heard the man," Sal Richmond said. "For Detective-Sergeant Paul Matthew it's still morning. It's rough, rock and roll in the morning." He bowed toward Paul, smiled blandly with strong white teeth.

"Thank you," Paul Matthew said.

"Oh, don't mention it, sir."

Sarcasm? Paul thought. *Or am I imagining? Who is this boy—my son's new friend? Or the girl, for that matter? Who are all these brand-new friends of my son?*

"Time to cut out," Sal Richmond said. "Let's go, Katie-gal."

"Okay by me," the girl said.

"I'll drive you to the station," Billy said.

"Big deal with the new jalopy," Sal said. "This Billy's some sport, hey?"

Paul Matthew went slowly to the kitchen. His wife greeted him with a kiss at a corner of his mouth. "Blame the entrance music on the beat generation," she said, "or the angry age, or, better, just don't blame anyone. Have breakfast."

He heard the boy's jalopy start up and roar off. He sat down, heavily, at the kitchen table. Cool-looking despite the heat of the day, his wife served him; fresh and clean; immaculate and fragrant in a bright-yellow sundress. *Mary,* he thought. *If ever a name fit a woman, Mary fit her. Beautiful and good. Married twenty-one years and I love her as much as I ever did.*

"More coffee?" she said.

"Please," Paul said.

She poured for him and poured for herself and sat near him.

"What is it, Paul?" she said softly.

"Nothing."

"Is it—business?"

"No."

"Then it's Billy, isn't it?" He made no answer. "Please tell me, Paul."

"Yes," he said. "Billy."

"What's happened between you two?"

"Nothing has happened between us." He stood up, paced, went to a window, squinted at the sky, scowled, came back, paced again. "Something's cockeyed with that kid lately."

"There's nothing wrong with Billy."

"Nothing wrong with these new friends of his? This running around wild? He's a different kid this summer."

"He's going into the Army in September, remember?"

"So? Does that give him a license to cut loose?"

"But he's *not* cut loose. He's having a bit of a fling, enjoying himself. He's eighteen, Paul. Eighteen."

"So? Eighteen. So at eighteen I asked him to go to college first, and then the Army. But not Billy. Billy wants the Army now"—he shrugged—"and who am I to stand in his way?"

"Is that why you're angry? Because he disobeyed your orders?"

"I didn't order. I suggested."

"But Paul, dear Paul, he's just like you. He has a will of his own, and principles of his own, and a mind of his own, and he's stubborn. Can you condemn him for that?"

"I'm not condemning him. Wow," he said, "how did we get into this? We just can't talk about that boy without getting into an argument." Clatteringly he collected the dishes and brought them to the sink. She washed and he wiped. "I'm worried," he blurted suddenly. "That's all. I'm not angry; I'm not condemning. Simply, I'm worried about him."

"Oh, no, please, Paul. There's nothing to worry about Billy. You know him as well as I do. Billy's a good boy."

He recoiled as though he had been spat upon. "Lord, how many times I've heard that." He dried his hands and paced again.

"Heard what?" she said. "Heard what?"

" *'He's a good boy!'* It's like a refrain written by a two-bit poet to be recited like a ritual by all the well-meaning parents all over the country."

"I don't care——"

" *'But he's a good boy! I know my son! He's a good boy!'* And they mean it, every living one of them. In the corridors of the courtrooms throughout the country, after their kids have been sentenced for murders, muggings, rapings, beatings, stealings, senseless attacks——these poor baffled parents stare at the lawyers with shocked eyes and they mumble, 'But he's a good boy, I know my boy, he's always been a good boy . . .' "

"Oh, no, please," she said. "I don't care about other people. I don't care about your courtrooms and corridors. I know my son."

"You approve of these friends, these people he's been running around with?"

"It's temporary——"

"Approve of the hours he's been keeping? Approve of the way he's been gallivanting in that broken-down car he bought? And where'd that money come from? Where'd he get the money to buy that car? The money he's been spending like dirt?"

She went to him, put her hands on his arms and held him. "May I, now? May I, please?"

"I'm sorry," he said. "I'm sorry I'm upsetting you."

"May I try to answer you?"

"Yes, Mary."

Her words came slowly. "For three years, each summer,

he's been away as a camp counselor. He's made money and he's saved it. Now he's through with school and he's going into the Army. So he's taken this summer off and he's having fun, his first grown-up summer in the city. He's a boy and he's having fun. What's wrong with that?"

"And these friends of his?"

"New people he's met. Part of the fun. Temporary. As temporary as this one wild summer of fun."

"And the money he's been spending?" Paul persisted. "The money for that jalopy?"

"What did it cost? A hundred and fifty dollars?"

"That's not tin."

"It's his own money. He has a right to a bit of a splurge."

Paul Matthew looked up at the kitchen clock. There was time."

"I'm going up for a look-see," he said.

"Look-see? For what?"

"His bank book."

A flush mottled her neck. "Are you sure you want to do that, Paul?"

"Yes. I'm sure."

Her blue eyes were wide and rigid and he could feel they were braced against tears. He avoided them. She stood motionless, silent and erect, as he quit the room.

He ran up the stairs, opened the door of the boy's room and closed it behind him. It was clean and spare: a boy's room. Immediately he went to a dresser, pulled a drawer, lifted shirts, looking for the book. *I ought to know where to look,* he thought. *I'm an old hand at knowing where to look.* He found the bank book and checked it. It contained thirteen hundred dollars. Not one penny had been withdrawn that summer. Certainly the boy received a weekly allowance, but just as certainly that allowance was insufficient to sustain him at the rate he had been going. And what about the car? He heard the downstairs door open and close and he heard the noise of Billy's rapid footsteps on the stairs. He kept the book in his hand. *If I'm checking on my son,* he thought, *I want my son to know it.* The boy burst into the room.

"Hi, Dad," he said. "Hot out."

"Hi," Paul Matthew said.

"Going to take a shower," Billy said. "Tennis this afternoon. And tonight, a real heavy date." He started, stopped. "What's that you're holding?"

"Your bank book."

A look of incredulity marked the boy's face like a welt after a slap. "What are you doing with my bank book, Dad?"

"Where'd you get the money?" Paul Matthew said.

"Money? What money?"

"The money you've been spending like dirt. The money to buy that car."

A flush rose to the boy's cheeks and remained like a stain. He shifted from foot to foot, but his eyes stayed on the bank book in his father's hand. "I . . . I won it."

"Won it? Where? How?"

"We went to the trotters, a gang of us."

"Real grown up, aren't you? So now it's racetracks, is it?"

"We only went once."

"It's against the law for you to make a bet. You're a minor."

"But it's not against the law for me to go."

Paul Matthew knew the law. It was part of his business to know the law. "No," he said, "you can go if you're over eighteen, but it's against the law for you to even approach one of those mutuel windows unless you're over twenty-one."

"I didn't approach the mutuel windows."

"Well, then, who the devil did?"

"I told you, a bunch of us went."

"Yes, a gang you said. Who?"

"Sal, Kate, other kids. Some of them were over twenty-one, and they did the betting for all of us. I got lucky. I hit a couple of real crazy long ones. I won."

"How much?"

"Three hundred and fifteen dollars."

Paul Matthew squinted, riffling the edge of the bank book. "And that's the money you've been spending?"

"Yes, sir."

"Then why didn't you tell us? Me? Your mother?"

The boy kicked a foot at the floor. "I . . . I didn't think you'd like it."

"Damn well right we wouldn't like it."

"And I didn't think you'd go looking in my bank book."

"Never mind that. You're telling me the truth now, aren't you?" The boy did not answer. "Aren't you, Billy?"

"You're insulting me, Dad."

"Oh, now we're on that pitch, are we?"

"I don't lie, Dad. Remember, I was brought up never to lie."

Paul Matthew shuffled uncomfortably. "Don't you consider withholding the truth—a lie?"

"Yes," the boy said. "And I admit it's been bothering me. But I weighed one side against the other, and I thought it wiser to let it lay, just not talk about it."

In silence Paul Matthew studied his son, and when he spoke his voice sounded muffled to him, sounded far away, sounded as though another were speaking and he were listening. "All right, Billy," he said. "I'll buy it. I'm sorry I blew up. Kids are crazy these days. Maybe I'm too jumpy. I think you made a mistake, a mistake in judgment, but bigger people than you have made mistakes in judgment."

"I just didn't think you'd go looking in my bank book."

"Do you blame me?"

"Yes," Billy said. "Yes, I blame you. There can't be two sets of rules. You brought me up a certain way; you've got to stick to the rules yourself."

Awkwardly Paul said, "What rules?" He knew what rules.

"You brought me up strict," Billy said. "Faith and integrity. No poking, no prying. Remember me, Dad? My things were mine. Your things yours. Mother's hers. I never opened your mail, or went to your pockets without permission, or even touched your gun. And you never touched my things, ever, without permission. Ever. So what's happened?"

"I'm sorry," Paul Matthew said. "Your old man's gotten

a little too jumpy for his own good, period. I'm sorry, Billy."

The boy moved away. He emptied the pockets of his clothes, made a loose heap of the contents on top of the dresser. He began to undress.

"Where'd you meet these people?" Paul Matthew said. "This Sal? Kate?"

"Jazz concert at one of the Village spots. They like the kind of music I like."

"You sweet on her?"

"A little bit," Billy said.

"She's Sal's girl, isn't she?"

Billy grinned. "Not for long, if I can manage it."

The boy went into the bathroom; the hiss of the shower filtered through. Paul Matthew looked at his reflection in the mirror and hated himself. He returned the bank book to the drawer; an object on the dresser caught his attention. It was a small rectangle of white paper, seemingly torn from a desk memorandum pad—with a diagram pencilled on it. The paper was cheap. The black printing, in a corner, stated: "RAMAREZ—518 WEST 19—MEMO." The diagram appeared to be that of the interior of a factory loft or a similar place of business. It was neat and expertly done. *Diagram,* Paul Matthew thought, and felt pain that was more than physical pain. *If you're an architect, a diagram can be a blueprint. If you're in the theatre, a diagram can be a floor plan. In my business, a diagram is a layout, and a layout is a sketch of premises cased for robbery.* He reversed the sheet of paper. A phone number was scrawled on the other side: "Delancey 3-7716."

The sound of the running water ceased.

"Billy!" Paul called.

"Yes, Dad?"

"I need a hunk of paper for some notations. There's a piece here with a phone number on it. May I have it?"

"Phone number?"

"A Delancey number."

"Oh, yeah. Sure you can have it."

"What's the phone number?"

"Blind date. The gal turned out to be a drip."

"Where'd you get the paper?"

"Search me. It was a party. Someone gave me the number."

"Where was the party?"

"One of the kids."

"Sal? Kate?"

"Search me. I wouldn't remember."

"Okay," Paul called.

Would he let me take the paper if it were a layout? Who knows? Kids are crazy these days, and he's a kid, like the rest of them, a kid, not a hardened criminal. Kids forget, kids get careless, kids don't remember. Or he may be telling me the truth—because another kid forgot, got careless, didn't remember. He may be telling me the exact truth—the number of a gal was jotted down on a sheet of paper that was a layout because another kid, a delinquent, forgot and was careless. Kids are kids. Kids aren't hardened criminals. But he has possession, and I'm a cop, and I know possession is prima facie, possession is part of evidence. But it could be that the thing isn't a layout at all. It could be I'm dreaming it up out of my own mind, steeped in rottenness. It could be my own rotten mind, reading evil into innocence.

"Okay," he called. "Thanks, Billy."

He quit his son's bedroom.

He closed the door behind him quietly.

Detective-Sergeant Paul Matthew walked up out of the subways, going to work, swirl-haze of fog moving in from the east. The precinct was on West 20th and he climbed the steps to the squad room without his customary wave at the desk. *Squad room,* he thought. *12th Detective Squad. Second floor of the 12th Precinct Police Station. One flight up to misery. One flight up to another world. One flight up to murder and mayhem and muggery. One flight up to an unending stream of thieves, marauders, arsonists, forgers, housebreakers, hoodlums, maniacs and murderers. Downstairs we book them, but here they're printed, and here they're questioned, and here the sordid stories roll out . . . here the raging effrontery, the calm lies, the daring ad-*

missions, the contemptuous silences . . . here the tears, the
hysterics, the leers . . . here in this old and ugly room, rust
on the bars of the windows, blistered paint on the green
walls.

He pushed through the gate of the iron railing and
offered an indiscriminate hello. Faber was at the typewriter,
asking questions of a frightened young man, tapping out
the answers. Ramsey was at the print shelf rolling the
fingers of a burly man with a broken nose. Carlson was
standing, staring out a window. The door to the Lieutenant's room was open, but the chair behind the desk
was empty. Paul said, to nobody, "Where's the Lieutenant?"

"Downtown," Carlson said. "Conference with the brass.
But you and me, we got orders. Same orders." Detective
Carlson was Detective-Sergeant Matthew's partner—a
broad-shouldered young man, four years a detective. "For
a guy like you, a brain-guy like you, for you it's a lousy
assignment. But we got to go, pal. A lot of footwork.
Twelve square blocks of it. All up and down."

"You mean they're still pushing that thing?"

"Yah. No break yet. Crazy old dame."

An elderly baby-sitter had disappeared—with the baby.
Ramsey looked up from the print shelf. "It ain't a kidnap-
ping. Yet. No note, no ransom deal, nothing. So it ain't for
the Federal boys. Strictly local, so far."

A woman answering to the description of the sitter had
been seen with a child answering to the description of the
missing child. She had been seen twice, acting strangely,
protectively; once in an east side playground and once in a
park on the lower west side. The word had come in, and
from there it had been routine.

"Up and down," Carlson said. "House to house, door to
door. A canvass job."

"How long does it figure this trip?" Paul said.

"About six hours. Let's go, pal."

They were past the gate when the typewriter clatter
ceased. Faber called: "Hey, Brains!"

Paul Matthew turned. "What?"

"The Loot left a message. Wants to see you when you

get back. It's on one of them loft jobs. Got a tip for tonight. Stoolie."

"A kid got stoned at a party and shot his face off," Carlson said. "The stoolie picked it up."

"What kid?" Paul Matthew said.

"No word on the kid, no word on nothing," Faber called. "Nothing, except the stoolie pointed it out for eleven o'clock tonight. 518 West 19th."

It was as though a fist had been smashed at his mouth.

"Where?"

"518 West 19th. First floor."

Carlson said, "Come on. Let's go, pal."

The clatter of the typewriter recommenced.

You are a cop and you are doing a canvass job with your partner. The heat sits all over you and the fog is squeezing in. And all the time there is a hammer going in your head, beating out the words: *Your son, your son, your son, your son.* You are a cop and you hate criminals and a crook is a crook and there is no compromise and even the old-time cops have called you a martinet—*but this is your son*—and you try, somehow, to deaden the turmoil inside of you. And you cannot.

When they reached 19th Street, Paul said, "I'm going up to that loft for a look-see. The Loot'll like it."

"I'm hungry," Carlson said. "You go, I'll grab a bite. I'll wait for you at the cafeteria over by 14th."

"You got a date," Paul Matthew said.

518 West 19th Street was near the corner of 11th Avenue. 518 was three stories high, an old building, the downstairs sheet-metal door without a lock. It was early dark now, fog-dark, the lights of 518 gloomily glistening, shrouded in fog. Paul Matthew pushed at the sheet-metal door and he was in a dank lobby, a small yellow bulb pouring faint illumination from a high ceiling. He climbed bent stairs to the first floor. There was one door, of wood, with a decrepit lock and an amateur-painted legend in white block letters: "RAMAREZ—LADIES' POCKETBOOKS." He walked in without knocking.

It was a large square room with an old-fashioned rolltop desk, a rickety swivel chair, four green filing cabinets, and an ancient safe. Up front, workers lined a long table. In the rear, a cutting machine loosed intermittent roars. He glanced about the room, remembering the diagram. *Good diagram,* he thought, *good piece of work. And a baby can open that safe with a teething ring.*

He asked for the boss and met Juan Ramarez, dark and pleasant. He told him he was a policeman, showed him his badge, informed him he was making a routine check of the neighborhood. Mr. Ramarez answered all his questions cheerfully and respectfully. Mr. Ramarez manufactured pocketbooks, he also sold retail to customers who came here to the shop, his employees worked piecework and were paid by the day, he kept a couple of hundred dollars in the safe at all times, there was no guard for the building, the downstairs light was on all night, he closed up shop at seven o'clock. Paul Matthew thanked him and departed.

He walked through fog toward 14th Street.

He entered a drug store and called home.

"Mary," he said. "Let me talk to Billy."

"He's not home yet, dear."

"Expecting him?"

"Of course. For supper."

"Give him a message, please."

"Paul, what's wrong? You sound—"

"Give him a message. He's to stay home tonight."

"But Paul—"

"He's not to leave the house. He's to stay home tonight. Strict orders."

"But why? What reason?"

"Strict orders," Paul Matthew said and hung up.

He sat slumped in the phone booth. He drew a hand-kerchief and wiped his face. *I'll straighten him out one way or another. Sooner or later, I'll straighten him out. But not tonight, please God, not at 518 West 19th Street, not on a job that's going to be my assignment. Sure I'm a cop, and I'm an honest cop, and I don't trade with criminals, but God, I'm human, and that stubborn kid's my son, he's my flesh and blood.* He wiped his face again, and his eyes. Then he went out of the phone booth, walked to the cafeteria and picked up Carlson.

They returned to the squad room at nine-thirty. The door to the Lieutenant's room was closed. Paul Matthew knocked and was admitted. The Lieutenant was a fleshy man with sharp eyes and a tired face.

"The brass has been eating my insides out all day," the Lieutenant said.

"That's part of the job of being a Lieutenant." Paul Matthew lit a cigarette.

"Thanks for the sympathy, Brains."

"You wanted to see me, Lieutenant?"

The Lieutenant showed stained teeth in a tired smile. "Always on the ball, aren't you? All right. Among other things the brass pounded me about these petty loft robberies we been having here on the west side. A few hundred dollars at a clip, but the insurance companies have been paying out, and they're kicking, and now the kick has come to me. Right in the pants. But we finally got a lead, a stoolie-lead. The boys tell you?"

"Yes."

"Go get him, Brains. My hunch, it's a one-kid operator who's racked himself up a good thing. You go get him, and I don't care if you take the whole squad with you."

"I'll go alone."

"Alone?" the Lieutenant asked.

"I looked the spot over this afternoon. I'll handle it myself."

"Okay. You're the brains. I'll have a couple of prowl cars in the vicinity."

"But keep them off that street."

"Okay. You're the brains."

There was a knock and Faber entered grinning. "From the teletype," he said and he handed across a sheet of paper.

The Lieutenant read quickly, scowled. "Sure. *We* do house-to-house—nothing. House-to-house on the *east* side —*they* find her." He looked up at Paul. "They picked up that old dame and the baby. Same old story—she was just cuh-razy about babies, had none of her own. They've got her in the boobyhatch and they're giving her dolls to play with." He sighed. "Okay, Brains. Take good care of that thing tonight. Let's get *one* damn credit mark racked up for us."

"Yes, sir."

"That's all."

Paul Matthew, in the squad room, clipped a flashlight to his belt, winked at Carlson, swung through the gate, went down the stairs and stepped out into fog. It was thick now —gasping-thick—headlights from the automobiles churning it up dim yellow. He could make out the mist-blurred forms of the people across the street, but he could not see who they were. He pondered the use of a squad car, decided against it—too much risk in this pea soup of fog. He went home by subway; the ride was slow and stalling and tedious; he walked quickly and impatiently from the station to his house. Mary was alone in the living room. "Tell Billy I want to talk to him now, right now, please."

"He's not here," Mary said.

"What?"

"He's not here." Her face was pale, strained.

"Where is he?"

"He went out."

"You told him I called?"

"Yes."

"Called special? Left strict orders?"

"Yes."

"Where'd he go?"

"He said he was going to the movies. That he had a date."

"Movies, huh?"

She came to him, put her arms around him, held him. "He was terribly upset, Paul."

"I'm sure he was."

"He wanted to know why—why you insisted he stay home. I told him you didn't say, that you called and left strict orders. He said he was always willing to listen to reason, but when there was no reason for 'strict orders,' he wouldn't obey them. He said he didn't believe in dictators, in being dictated to. Paul, please, you've got to get it through your head he's not a baby any more. He's a man, with spirit; he's like you . . ."

"Like me, is he?"

"Like you, like you . . ."

He pulled free from her grasp. "All right. I've got to go now."

"Can't you stay home? We'll wait for him together. We'll talk it out, the three of us."

"I can't," Paul Matthew said. "I've got to go to work."

He arrived at 19th Street and 11th Avenue at five minutes after eleven. There was a deep hallway across the street from 518, a streetlamp burning outside of it. He went there and waited.

If he was prompt, he's up there right now. And he'll be out within fifteen minutes. If he wasn't prompt, then I'll see him go in. But I'm not going to try to stymie it any more, not now, not for him, not for anybody. It's out of my hands now. I asked him to stay home, strict orders. I thought I could work it out that way. But he didn't stay home. Okay. I'm a cop not a social worker. I'm a cop out on a job of work. I'm here to catch a thief. That's why I'm here. That's my job of work. He gulped, swallowed dryly, peered from the deep recess of the dark hallway.

Fog swirled around his streetlamp. Occasionally, a person went by, wraithlike, wrapped in fog. He starved for a cigarette but he did not smoke. He waited in the dark hallway, moving from foot to foot, and then he realized that the wet-cold in the palm of his hand was the butt of his gun. He held it pressed against his thigh.

I am waiting for my son with a gun in my hand. I tried, Mary. I went as far as a guy like me can go. And now I'm waiting for Billy with a gun in my hand. Remember him, Mary? Growing up, he wouldn't tell a lie for nothing, his old man's pride, a rugged honest kid, never told a lie, not Billy, not my Billy-boy, rugged and honest and a stickler for the truth, because his old man was crazy about the truth, because his old man was in a business where he'd learned to hate a sniveling liar. And now Billy's grown, and Billy's out on his own, and old Paul Matthew, old Brains the martinet, old Paul Matthew is waiting for his son with a gun in his hand.

There was a movement at 518. The sheet-metal door opened.

A figure emerged. Fog wisped around it.

Paul Matthew raised his gun but he did not shoot.

"Stop!" he called. "Stop!"

Fog blanketed echoes of his voice.

The figure whirled, hesitated, ran.

No! He's coming toward me! Go the other way, Billy! No! No! Go the other way!

Paul Matthew, an experienced cop, stepped out of the dark hallway and stood under the light of the streetlamp.

"Stop!" he called. "Stand still!" Running feet skidded to a halt. The figure stood stock-still. "I'm coming for you!" Paul Matthew called. "Stay where you are!" He moved forward slowly, murmuring as in prayer: "Please stay where you are."

And now, twistingly, the figure turned, lurched; and the feet were running again.

"Stop!" Paul put a bullet into the air. "Stop!"

Feet ran. Paul leveled the gun. He held his arm out stiff. He pulled the trigger. A scream came back like that of an animal. The figure dropped in the gutter. Shufflingly, gun hanging in hand, Paul Matthew dragged himself forward.

The boy lay prone, half in the gutter, half on the sidewalk, uttering low moaning sounds. Paul pulled his flashlight. From far off, he heard the sound of a siren.

He bent to the boy and turned him over.

Sal Richmond blinked glazed eyes.

"Hi," Sal Richmond said. The eyes closed.

Paul Matthew touched the boy's throat, feeling for a pulse. The eyes opened, the lids flickered. "Do you know me?" Paul Matthew said. "Do you recognize me?"

"Detective-Sergeant Paul Matthew," the boy said. He quivered, biting back a sob. "It hurts," he said.

"They're coming," Paul Matthew said. "They'll be here soon."

The boy fought for breath. "Hurts," he wheezed. "Hurts so much. Up on the back. Like by the lungs somewhere."

"Easy, kid," Paul Matthew said. He sat on the edge of

the sidewalk. He drew the boy to him, put his head in his lap, used the flat of his palm to wipe perspiration from the boy's forehead.

"Thanks," the boy said.

The sound of the siren was nearer. Paul Matthew raised his gun, fired twice.

"What are you doing?" the boy said.

"Giving them a better idea where we are. They'll come quicker."

"Thanks," the boy said.

"Did you make a diagram?" Paul Matthew said.

"Diagram?" The boy's voice was a cackle, dry, strange, old.

"Of 518."

"Yes. Staked the joint. Worked a day under a phony name."

"What did you do with the diagram?"

"Don't know. Once I had it studied, I had it made. Who needs diagrams?" He gasped, his body arching upward, held motionless in a vise of pain. "Oh, man, that hurts." The body convulsed, fell back; the breathing was shallow and rapid. And then quite simply he said, "I'm going to die, Sergeant." And he smiled, sweetly, and it was a boy's face, a face of innocence. "Thief," he said suddenly. "No-good, wise-guy, punk thief. I ought to be proud, huh?"

"Your folks?" Paul said.

"Got no folks. Got an uncle somewhere." He winced. "Man, I wish it would stop hurting."

"They'll be here any minute."

"Hold me. Please hold me. Hold me tight. Please hold me."

Paul Matthew held him. The boy whimpered, grew quiet.

"Sal."

"Yes?" The boy roused.

"Was Billy mixed in any of this—these stealings?"

"Billy? You kidding, Sergeant?"

"I'm not kidding."

"The only stealing Billy ever done—he stole my girl, is all. Stole my girl." The boy tried for a smile, but his lips stiffened. He looked away.

"Forgive me," Paul Matthew whispered.

Sal Richmond turned his head in the policeman's lap. Tears brimmed in his eyes. "Look, I ain't got nothing against you, Mr. Matthew. You done your job—so you done your job. There ain't nothing for me to forgive." He sagged, lay helpless, an involuntary whine like a thin whistle in his throat.

Paul Matthew cradled the boy's head, held him close, very close, his body a shield around him.

"Please forgive me," Paul Matthew whispered to nothing, to no one, to fog. "Forgive me, Billy. Mary, forgive me." He looked out to nothing, to no one, to fog. "We'll talk it out, Billy-boy. I'll explain it to you and we'll get it straightened away. I'll—"

"You forgive me," said the boy in his lap. The face veered upward, high, strained, exposed, naked; a fervor was in his eyes.

"Easy, kid," Paul Matthew said.

"You shot me," the boy said. "You killed me. I'm dead."

"No, no. Easy, now. Easy does it."

"Me. Wise-guy, smart aleck, crook, thief. I'm going to die from that hole you put in me, I know it, I know it." The head fell back. The voice, a frail rasp, was a reverent supplication. "Please, before I die, I need you to forgive me, I need you." Desperately the boy pleaded. "Please, please, can you understand?"

"I understand," Paul Matthew said.

"Please say it—please say it loud so I can hear—please say *you* forgive *me*."

"I forgive you," Paul Matthew said.

"Thanks—thanks for forgiving me," the boy said. "Thanks."

And the thief wept unashamedly.

And the policeman wept unashamedly.

And the loud wail of the siren was upon them.

A Crime Worthy of Me
Hal Dresner

CLOSE YOUR EYES and turn around, please, Arnold,"
Mr. Cumberby said.

I closed my eyes and turned around, feeling like a sleep-
walker, and heard Mr. Cumberby turning the dial to open
the safe.

Click-click-click-click.

Sixteen right, I thought.

Click-clickety-clickety-click.

Eleven left, I smiled evilly.

Clickety-clickety-click-click-click.

"Twenty-six right," I said out loud; but fortunately for
me Mr. Cumberby was practically deaf.

"All right, Arnold," he said. "You may turn back now."

I turned back and took a long, loving look at $110,-
584.00, all stacked in neat little bundles, like the baseball
cards in my bedroom; and Mr. Cumberby carefully added
another small pile, which, I knew, brought the total up to
$110,708.00. Then he closed the door of the safe with a
thwank!

"Finished for today," he said. "It's five-thirty now so
you can be going. I'll be working late for another hour."

"Yes, sir," I said and cast a baleful glance at the safe,
sitting like a fat black toad, and at Mr. Cumberby, toadlike
in his own way, struggling to his feet. He was really a
kindly old man who reminded me of my grandfather; if he
hadn't I think I would have clipped him on his kindly old
head right then, twirled the safe dial to those digits I knew
better than my Social Security number, crammed those little
packets of green into the paper bags I had hidden in my
desk (I had forty-three of them by then, brought in one a

day, inconspicuously containing my mother's own special brand of tuna salad, egg salad and cream-cheese-and-olive sandwiches) and then I would be out on Murray Street looking no more suspicious than any of the other Bainesville shoppers on their way home with their groceries.

That had been Plan One, inspired by my first week as junior clerk in the Bainesville Home Finance and Loan Company, but as the summer progressed I had discarded it as unworthy of me and gone on to more ingenious scheming. I rediscarded it as I turned from Mr. Cumberby and walked to my desk.

The office of the Bainesville Home Finance and Loan Company was one L-shaped room with a single door and no windows. Mr. Cumberby's desk and the safe were at the short line of the L, obscured from mine by the corner; the longer line contained the desk of Miss Framage, the two-thousand-year-old senior clerk, my own cubicle, a wooden railing (which I had practiced hurdling for the crucial moment), two waiting benches and then the door. There was also an assortment of filing cabinets, a water cooler, air conditioner and a hat rack strategically placed about, but these had no great bearing on my plans and I had omitted them from the sixty or seventy maps I had drawn.

In short, it was a building built to be robbed—but only by the most brilliant and daring of master thieves, an uncanny craftsman of the illegal of whom the world would certainly say, "he could have succeeded in any chosen field" but whom the world would never know was Bainesville's own beloved Arnold Handleman.

So far, however, I had only managed to draw maps and hide forty-three paper bags; and, of course, discover the combination to the safe by listening intently to the number of clicks. (Once, just to check my calculations, I had opened my eyes and turned around to watch Mr. Cumberby while he was applying the combination. Needless to say, I had been correct to the digit.) Mr. Cumberby was the only one entrusted with that combination and I hoped he would be able to clear himself after the crime was discovered. At the moment, his safety seemed assured since I had no idea how I would accomplish my heinous deed.

I had, however, eliminated several courses. I would not kill or harm Mr. Cumberby, mainly because I was kind and humane as I was brilliant and daring, but short of killing or harming him, I did not see how I could accomplish the crime in his presence and still nurture any real hope of escaping punishment. Of course there was a serum which, when introduced into the bloodstream, induced permanent amnesia. I had been perfecting it in my bathroom laboratory. But at last report, the serum was not completely foolproof and its single test case, on my dog Ambrose, had only caused Ambrose to lose the ability to wag his tail for several hours. That would hardly do for Mr. Cumberby.

Thus, the crime would have to be performed in secret. Once inside the building alone, it would only be a matter of scant minutes before the safe was open and the money residing in my sandwich bags. I could, of course, hide in the office now but—

"Don't forget to close the door when you leave," Mr. Cumberby called.

—then I could not get out; because the door was plated steel which locked immediately when closed and Mr. Cumberby had the only key.

Although anyone with enough wax in their ears could make an impression of the lock and have a duplicate key made, there was also a burglar alarm. Mr. Cumberby set it when he left each night and it went off, very loudly, the next time the door was opened by anyone. Bill Christie, the cop on the beat, waited for Mr. Cumberby at nine each weekday morning with the three sets of keys that unlocked the box and killed the alarm—but not before it had sounded for five minutes, irritating everyone on Murray Street and usually waking me with the news that I was late for work again. If the alarm was disconnected before it went off, then the door could not be opened at all.

It was a cunning little setup all right which posed a challenge worthy of me, the king of thieves, and I had spent the better part of my summer pondering it. But now, as I walked home each evening, more and more leaves fell on my shoulders reminding me that the summer was almost over and in two weeks I would be leaving for Norton

Junior College, forced to abdicate my thieves' throne emptyhanded.

I said goodnight to Mr. Cumberby, dispiritedly closed the door behind me, heard the lock catch, and was out on Murray Street in the jostle of Bainesville shoppers, looking as inconspicuous as planned.

At the corner of the Bainesville Home Finance and Loan Company building (solid brick and mortar) was the office mail slot (steel planted in cement). It was only about six inches wide and three feet off the ground but large and high enough to serve as an eye-hole and many were the dark nights I had spent peering into that blackness and plotting vainly. I lifted the flap now to take another look at the scene of the crime of the century. The light from Mr. Cumberby's lamp dimly illuminated the office and I viewed it as it would be seen by the police and the awed crowds the morning after; not a drawer handle smudged with telltale fingerprints, not a paper clip mislaid. It would astound them how the thief had gotten in and out without leaving a trace. Right then, it astounded me.

I lowered the flap quietly and strolled on. Discarded Plan B was, admitting my own vulnerability, to seek the aid of an experienced burglar to help gain exit from the building. As the brains, I would take the lion's share of the booty but I shrank from the notion for reasons which included the possibility that my witless accomplice might decide to sell me out when he was apprehended for another, less clever, crime; or, greedy and dissatisfied with his cut, he might decide to blackmail me later; or, being as vile and ungrateful as the general run of criminal, he might decide to murder me on the spot.

A final, more practical objection was that Bainesville did not abound with underworld characters and the shadiest person I knew was Max Derrick, who purportedly bet on Bainesville High School baseball games.

I walked on up Murray Street, and the falling leaves brought thoughts of Norton J. C. and the uses to which I would put my plunder. Although I had agreed to allow my parents to pay my tuition and living expenses, there were a few extracurricular items I would need, such as a luxurious bachelor apartment with thigh-thick rugs, wall-to-wall stereo and a bar that piped liquor into any room; a pleasant place where, when not absorbed in my studies, I would dally away idle hours with coeds of all types and sororities. Also, there was an aching need for a lynx-sleek sports car, possibly in chrome with black paint trim, and a wardrobe replete with monogrammed shirts, houndstooth jackets, smoking robes, butter-colored ascots and sapphire cuff links.

The remainder of my loot would be invested in carefully chosen securities which would so pyramid in value during the next two years that immediately upon graduating from Norton, I would retire, set up a trust fund for my parents, and spend my declining years in a small but ornate villa within walking distance of the Riviera. Later, maybe twenty years hence, when my investments had matured a hundred-fold, I might decide to assuage the pangs of guilt and return the original loan to the Bainesville Home Finance and Loan Company with a cryptic little note; or, perhaps I might indulge the more charitable side of my nature by donating a piddling sum to my Alma Mater so that they might establish the Arnold Handleman School of Finance.

All of these were truly well-thought-out lines of endeavor but, the leaves reminded me, if I was to be Norton's most successful graduate I would have to find a workable plan tonight——for it was Friday, the Bainesville Home Finance and Loan Company was closed over the weekend and on Monday began B.H.F.L.C.'s annual Fall Money Special, which meant that daily, from then on, the money for my rug and roadster and smoking robe would be ladled out to all the town indigents to feed their mewling children.

So tonight would be my last chance to abscond with the big money; there was still an hour more when Mr. Cumberby would be in the office and I could gain at least temporary access to the building and I was not willing to shrug off this opportunity without a final brainstorming session. The gain was worth the risk of my father's rancor when I returned home late for dinner again, so determinedly I strode into George Gibbon's Drugstore and curled into an empty booth near the magazine rack.

"I don't suppose you want anything else," George said as he brought me a glass of water.

I shook my head.

"Well, try not to use more than one napkin," he said. "And don't touch the magazines. I can't sell them after you crack the bindings."

"They won't lie flat unless I crack the bindings," I informed him.

"You'll be lying flat if you crack them," he said with customary wit.

Wearily, I waved him away. Another of my early plans was to set fire to George's place in the hope that Mr. Cumberby, on hearing the alarm, would rush to George's aid with a cup or two of water from the office cooler; in his haste to help, he would leave the office door open, of course. I had abandoned it as impractical, due to Mr. Cumberby's poor hearing, but now I reconsidered the idea for spite. The thought of the flames gnawing away at George's new counter and gobbling up his cheap plastic booths was a pleasant one but it made me thirsty. I drank some of my water and stared at the glass meditatively.

Water, I thought. Now if the office water cooler suddenly backed up and began to flood, deaf or not, Mr. Cumberby would certainly notice it and run for help. Even if he closed the door behind him, I might just be able to accomplish my deed in the crowd and confusion. The difficulty, of course, would be obtaining a map of the Bainesville water system, digging down to the right pipe and then devising a hose and pump mechanism to attach to the cooler line and start the fountain overflowing.

The clock on the wall over George read twenty to six. I had fifty minutes. Not enough time.

Twenty minutes later, the clock read six and I had, in order, discarded schemes to drill from the roof through the two floors above the loan office; to burrow down from the top floor where Mr. Baklivia, the burly superintendent, lived; and to excavate from the second floor which contained the Pete Enciso Dance Studio that held Friday night parties.

"Hey, George," I called. "Are there lots of sewers in this town?"

"Sure. Sappley's place," he said, naming his despised competitor.

That wasted another precious minute. I could feel the thigh-thick rug being pulled out from under me; the monogrammed shirts slipping from my back; tearfully, I imagined my lynx-sleek roadster reverting to my eight-year-old bike while dozens of coeds blew good-bye kisses and faded into mist.

Face it, Handleman, I said to myself. *You may be daring and brilliant and able to succeed in any chosen field, but you're also licked.*

I faced it and surreptitiously reached behind me for the latest issue of *Uncanny Detective Stories*. Quietly, I cracked the binding and with resignation turned to:

INSPECTOR McGRONSKEY'S
TOUGHEST CASE
An Inspector McGronskey Story
by Lester Swadding

Commander of Criminal Investigation Harberson was sitting in his office thinking of Inspector Mc-Gronskey when in walked the famed Scotland Yard ace himself.

"Well, well," said Harberson taking a pull on his meerschaum, "this is a coincidence, McGronskey. I was just about to call you. The Schindler Necklace was stolen last night and I've assigned you to head the investigations."

"I suspected as much," McGronskey said wryly, settling his bulk in a tan leather chair and taking out his black briar. "And I came in to tell you that I cracked the Schindler Necklace Case not ten minutes ago. The priceless heirloom is back in Lady Schindler's vault and the thief is now in Blackamoor Jail awaiting trial.

"How incredible!" said Harberson. "You must tell me about it."

"Of course," said the great detective, and he drew a

packet of Burley-Burbage from his coat, offered it to the Commander and the two men pulled their chairs closer and began to fill their pipes as McGronskey talked.

"It was a strange case," he began, "and in many ways my toughest one. Perhaps most unusual of all was the twist of circumstance which enabled me to apprehend the criminal before I was aware a crime had been committed. It began last evening. I was home alone, reading a mystery novel, when I heard a knock at the door. I answered it and found a short, lean young man who suavely apologized for disturbing me, explaining that his car had broken down in front of my house and he wished to use my phone to call for repairs. I did not recognize him at first but his polished Continental manner aroused my suspicions and after the call had been made, I accompanied him back to his car. It was then that I spied the famous Schindler Necklace lying on the seat. Casually, I questioned the man and he confessed to the theft immediately. It was André Gennaud, that incredibly daring and brilliant young safecracker whose series of seemingly impossible robberies have plagued police all over Europe for many months now."

"Good Grief!" said Harberson. "What a brilliant catch!"

Terrific, I thought, and turned the page.

McGronskey nodded his thanks modestly. "I thought so too, at the time," he said, "but I was also interested as to how Gennaud had accomplished his ingenious crime. So I drove to the Schindler mansion. It was past twelve but all the lights were burning and the great house was in a state of festive upheaval, for one of Lady Schindler's famous masquerade balls was in progress. Beautiful women and courtly gentlemen were dancing and drinking with abandon, all costumed in gay medieval attire. There were princes and knights, court ladies, jesters and, of course, Lady

Schindler herself, dressed in the style of Marie Antoinette. I entered the ballroom by way of the garden, the music stopped, and I announced that the famous Schindler Necklace had been stolen!"

"What an uproar that must have made," said Harberson chuckling and tamping down on his meerschaum.

"Indeed," said McGronskey. "Before I had an opportunity to announce that the necklace had been recovered, Lady Schindler had fainted in the center of the great hall."

McGronskey took advantage of the Commander's surprise to tamp down on his black briar. "It seems," he continued, "that Lady Schindler had seen her necklace safe in its vault not an hour before. Indeed, all of her guests had seen it since she had taken them down to her underground vault room to view the highly publicized bauble. Of course, I immediately surmised that Gennaud, costumed as one of the guests, was among the party; but that was the easiest part."

"Oh, I don't know," I mused dryly as I turned the next page.

Harberson puffed on his meerschaum, keeping his eyes and attention fixed on McGronskey.

"As you probably know," said the detective, "the Schindler Necklace is kept in a locked safe in an underground vault room which has but one door and no windows. The key to that door is kept at all times by Lady Schindler herself and although it would be possible to have a duplicate key made, it would serve the culprit little purpose, for there is also a burglar alarm which, when set, sounds as soon as the door is opened again by anyone. The alarm can be turned off only from the inside, providing the person has the three keys necessary to unlock the box, but once the alarm is disconnected before it has sounded, the door cannot be opened from either side."

"An incredible system," said Harberson.

"But not incredible enough," said McGronskey. "Now I assumed that Gennaud entered the vault room with the other guests and hid there, unbeknownst to Lady Schindler, when the others departed. Lady Schindler herself was the last to leave. After making sure the necklace was in the locked safe, she set the alarm and locked the vault room door. Now we know that Gennaud is an expert safecracker so the necklace itself posed no great problem. But once inside that room, how could he get out without activating the alarm?"

McGronskey paused and began to scrape the bowl of his briar with his housekey. "In order to solve that problem," he said quietly, "I had Lady Schindler lock *me* in that vault room."

"Bravo!" said Harberson. "Brilliant. But how did you get out?"

McGronskey peered at him, smiling. "Guess," he said slyly.

"You drilled through the door," ventured Harberson.

"No. Remember, I was obliged to use the same means of escape as Gennaud and it would have been impossible for him to hide the necessary drilling equipment on his person. In addition, I found no signs of destruction when I entered the vault room."

"You had an accomplice, then?" guessed Harberson.

"No."

"False ceiling."

"No."

"Sliding panel."

"No."

"I'll take that magazine," said George.

"No!" I cried.

But he already had it in one beefy hand and was reaching for me with the other. "Out! I warned you about the bindings. Now, out!"

"No, George. You don't understand. Just let me finish the story."

"I understand fine. I say okay and then it turns out that the story is continued for the next four months."

I certainly hoped he was wrong; but it had happened. On several occasions, to my fury and consternation, McGronskey and Harberson had sat around milking one story for months on end; they never ate, they never slept, they just sat and smoked an endless supply of Burley-Burbage from March to October. I suppose that some readers enjoy being kept in a suspended state of agitation but for myself, I like the cases open and shut and no tricky endings.

I did not bother to explain that preference to George. All I said was: "Listen George, if that story is complete in this issue, I'll buy the magazine."

He looked mildly stunned and I looked up at the clock and saw it was 6:15.

"Well, what about it?" I asked impatiently.

"All right," he said, "but *I'll* look to see if it's complete. I don't believe you."

I ignored this slander. "We'll both look," I suggested and the two of us bent over the magazine while my delicate fingers turned the pages.

It was complete; just two verbose pages later (which made it not only McGronskey's toughest case but also his shortest). I saw "THE END" and had time to greedily devour the agonizing paragraph above it:

> "So that's how it was done," Harberson said. "Brilliant, McGronskey. Simply brilliant."

Before George had the book crunched in his fist, the other hand outstretched for his money.

"Here, here, here," I said, doling out a handful of change.

"You gave me too much," he counted.

"Keep it. For the cracked bindings. Just give me my magazine." The clock on the wall read 6:17.

"Take it easy," said George, but he held the book. I made a grab for it but he whisked it behind his back, grinning apishly—if that is not giving him too much evolutionary credit. "You really want this pretty bad, don't you?" he asked.

"I'm a big mystery fan," I said.

"That so? Well, let me see what's so good about this McGromish character? He's got a few girl friends maybe?"

"No, he's too stalwart," I said. That was a mistake. George didn't know what "stalwart" meant.

"Yeah?" he leered broadly. "I like to read about guys like that," and holding the book high above his head, he began to peruse for suspected lewdities.

The clock read 6:18 and I stopped grabbing and whirled around to the rack for another copy of *Uncanny*. After all, I was entitled to one; I had paid for it; it wasn't stealing. And even if it was, what did I, the Bainesville André Gennaud, care about le petit larceny?

Naturally, there were no other copies of *Uncanny* on the rack. Bainesville is big McGronskey territory. George was probably holding the only copy of *Uncanny* left in town, maybe in the world.

The clock read 6:20 and I resumed my grabbing.

"Okay, okay," said George. "I couldn't find any sex. You want me to wrap this up for you?"

"Don't bother. I can read it better if it's not wrapped."

"No bother," he said maliciously. "I'll be glad to do it. After all, it's the first time you ever bought a magazine here. That's an occasion. I'll go see if I've got some birthday wrapping."

There were no other customers in the place so George had nothing better to do than give me his personal attention. He tramped into the back room while the clock said 6:22, 6:23, 6:24, about that quickly.

At 6:25 he came out, beaming, and handed me my present. It was wrapped in pink and gold paper patterned with candles and tied, tightly, with a baby-blue ribbon.

"And many, many, more." George shouted as I ran out into the street, tearing at the wrapping.

A block later I was running and reading back to the office.

"Well, well," said Harberson musing. He rubbed the bowl of his pipe against his nose. "Let me think for a moment."

"Take your time," said McGronskey.

The clock on the Bainesville Bank building said 6:27.

"No special equipment of any kind?" Harberson asked.

He already told you that, I thought angrily.

"No," said McGronskey, "I had nothing but the average possessions of an average man. My wallet, my comb and my handkerchief."

Check, check, check.

"But was it a special wallet in some way?" Harberson asked slyly.
McGronskey suppressed a smile. "No, I'm afraid you're on the wrong track, Commander. Gennaud and I effected our escapes using only common sense."

"And daring and brilliance," I added, stuffing the magazine in my pocket for I had reached the office. But was Mr. Cumberby still there?
I rang the bell. No answer.
I thumped on the door with both fists. No reply.
I yelled, "Mr. Cumberby, Mr. Cumberby!" Nothing.
The clock on the Bainesville Bank building read: 6:29. He had to be there, I reasoned. If a man says he's going to work for an hour beginning at 5:30, he must still be working at 6:29. I banged on the door for another minute before I remembered that Mr. Cumberby was almost deaf. Of course he was still in there; he just couldn't hear me. So I ran down to the mail slot. His desk light was still burning but the corner of the office obscured him from me.
"Mr. Cumberby!" I shouted (as well as you can shout into a hole about six inches wide). "Mr. Cumberby, it's me, sir, it's Arnold!"
"Arnold?" he said curiously.
"Yes sir!" I yelled.

"Arnold? I thought you left long ago."

"I did, Mr. Cumberby! I'm outside! By the mail slot!"

"Oh?" He sounded puzzled. "No other delivery tonight, is there?"

"I don't believe so!" I shouted. "But I'd like to come in for a minute! I forgot something!" I could picture him shaking his head good-naturedly. Fortunately, part of my adroit planning had included a whole summer's portrayal of a village idiot. Never knowing when such a reputation might come in handy, during the past two months I had been careful to misfile papers, erroneously compute interest rates and, at one time or another, pretend to fall against and successfully knock over anything that was movable; I had also forgotten sundry personal items from time to time in order to set up an occasion such as this. Twice, my overall performance had been so convincing as to put me on the brink of unemployment, but now it was finally paying off.

"All right, Arnold," Mr. Cumberby said. "I'll be right there."

I watched until I saw him shuffle around the bend in the office and then I ran to meet him at the door.

He opened it part way and peered at me, smiling. "Now what did you forget this time? Not your shoe again?"

"No, sir. My fountain pen." The lie came to me automatically.

"And you need it tonight?"

"Yes sir. My mother wants me to write some letters for her. It's very important."

"Why can't she write them herself?" he asked.

"Because she hasn't got my pen," I said, uncertain where this line of questioning was leading.

Mr. Cumberby looked confused too, and again my village-idiot planning saved the day. "Very well," he said sighing and moved out of the way, enough to let me in.

I trotted over to my desk and started to rummage through the drawers while Mr. Cumberby watched from the door. It was not the location I had planned for him.

"I can't seem to find it," I said. "But I'd better keep on looking or my mother will kill me." I searched through another drawer convincingly. "She gave me that pen as a graduation present," I added for no reason.

Mr. Cumberby looked at me with what, in the dim light, seemed like a mixture of pity and disgust. Then he plodded around the corner to his desk. "Just don't forget to close the door when you leave," he said wearily.

I told him I wouldn't forget and rattled the drawers for another minute before I shouted: "I found it, Mr. Cumberby! It was under my rubber bands!" and still at top volume: "I'm going now! Goodnight!"

He said goodnight, I hurdled the railing, opened the door, let it slam and scampered back and hunched under my desk. It was like a small cave in there but light enough to continue reading. Harberson was still not even warm.

"I'm afraid I give up, McGronskey," the Commander said, knocking the tobacco from his pipe.

"Oh, come now," chided his ace detective. "If Gennaud and I could figure out an escape, surely you, with all your years of criminal experience, can deduce a solution. Here, let me review the facts for you. You're locked in a vault—"

Mr. Cumberby's light went out and I heard him scraping across the floor. It was dead quiet and I was particularly careful not to make a sound although it was unlikely he would have heard me if I had decided to dance behind him with tambourines. But this was no time for foolishness and I resisted a strong impulse to jump from my hiding place and shout "Boo!" just to see his expression. Instead, I held my breath, heard him turn off the air conditioner, set the alarm, open the door, close it and then the lock turned with a heartwarming click!

I stayed hunched under the desk for another minute, for good measure, and then leaped out—only ten minutes and two pages away from being Bainesville's wealthiest minor.

Since there were no windows in the office, I could have turned on a light, all the lights if I cared to, but I was shrewd enough to consider the reflection, or something, showing up the air-conditioner duct where it might be seen by someone above; also, there was the mail slot where, for all I knew, some Arnold-come-lately might be peering and plotting at that very moment. It was a time for that extra gram of caution that separates the residents of the Riviéra from those of Blackamoor Jail. I decided to risk only a match.

A search of my pockets and desk drawers later led me to believe I woud not even risk that. Grimly I recalled my wily purchase of a pocket flashlight when I first began preparing for my night of crime. I had been careful enough to don a bizarre costume (bandana, cowboy shirt, bathing suit, sneakers) which no one would associate with my conservative nature; then I had bicycled six miles to neighboring Tipton where I bought the flashlight under a fictitious name. Now it was lying useless, concealed in a sock, beneath my mattress at home.

It was a dark moment for true genius and as I considered it, from overhead came the seductive strains of a tango, followed by the stamping and clicking of feet. The dance party had started.

It was small consolation to note the similarity between my situation and that of the real André Gennaud, locked in his dark underground vault while Lady Schindler and her guests frolicked above him. Of course my overhead revelers would be only the town's spinsters swaying and lurching about in the arms of Pete Enciso and his company. Several of my old high school teachers would be there, I supposed, kicking up their high-buttoned shoes and certainly Miss Framage for whom the dance was life itself. She was probably stamping with special vigor on the spot above her desk.

Miss Framage smoked, I then remembered quite naturally; she smoked filtered mentholated little cigarettes in a long plastic holder but it was, technically, smoking and it required matches. Before another two tango beats had passed, I was over at Miss Framage's desk and holding a book of her matches in my hand.

Then I too did a little dance step: one and two and over to the safe, then one and two and back to Miss Framage's desk; I had forgotten my gloves.

Miss Framage, however, had not forgotten hers—but audacious André Handleman was a master of improvisation and he artfully wrapped his handkerchief about one hand, two of Miss Framage's tissues about the other and bound the ends to his wrists with Scotch tape.

With some awkwardness, I managed to light a match as the music above me changed to a mambo, complete with maracas and castinets and I accompanied it on the safe dial.

Pedro Handleman and his Swinging Safe. Sixteen right, eleven left, twenty-six right, cha-cha-cha. Click, turn and open!

I was back at my desk for the sandwich bags, back at the safe for the stuffing. Oscar Handleman, caterer for private parties.

Unfortunately, I had more bags than the Bainesville Home Finance and Loan Company had money so seventeen ex-sandwich holders went back into my desk drawer. I would dispose of them on Monday which, I decided, would be a good time to tender my notice. A timely little speech began to compose itself in my mind.

Mr. Cumberby, Miss Framage, assorted customers of the Bainesville Home Finance and Loan Company and friends: it grieves me to have to address you today when I know that you, like myself, are still shocked and astounded by the recent discovery of the most lucrative and perfect robbery in Bainesville history. I only wish that I had some words of solace to offer but instead I am afraid I must only add to your woes by tendering my resignation as junior clerk.

As some of you are perhaps aware, I shall soon be departing to attend Norton Junior College and it has recently come to my attention that there are some matters of personal preparation which require my immediate efforts. . . . Lest you think ill of me for deserting you in your hour of need . . .

I would have ample time to finish the rest over the weekend, if a speech of resignation was needed at all. There was a good chance that after Monday the Bainesville Home Finance and Loan Company might have to economize a bit and perhaps cut down on its payroll, if not close its doors altogether.

With the money safely bagged and the safe closed, I devoted a solemn moment to concern for my co-workers, Mr. Cumberby and Miss Framage. It was likely that Mr. Cumberby, capable as he was, would be able to secure another position in the field of finance. A happy thought was that he might get a job with the Bainesville Bank, in which case next summer might see us fellow workers once more. As for Miss Framage—well perhaps her dancing would take her somewhere.

But then it was time to devote a moment to my own well-being. It was Library Hour.

With the sacks of money at my feet and another of Miss Framage's matches in hand, I plumped myself on the floor against the water cooler and prepared to memorize the instructions for my escape. McGronskey was still where I had left him, reviewing the situation. I felt amply familiar with it and skipped to the next paragraph.

> Harberson chewed on the stem of his meerschaum for a moment before he said: "I'm afraid I'm stumped, McGronskey. Tell me, how did you manage to get out of that locked vault room?"
>
> McGronskey smiled warmly. "It was really quite simple, Commander. Naturally, I couldn't attempt to open the door or tamper with the alarm but that did not stop me from . . ."

The page ended there and eagerly my eyes went to the top of the next one.

> Rick Raft lit a cigarette and smiled at Chief of Police Murchison. "Murder?" he asked.

George, of course, had ripped out the last page of McGronskey.

I still wasn't licked. Granted, it was a temporary set-back but I still had the telephone and my own daring. Now it was becoming a crime really worthy of me.

First I made a few friendly calls to local people who I thought might be mystery fans. Some weren't home and the others hadn't read the story. I advised them to rush right out and get it but I know they won't; people never do. Then I called Sappley's Drugstore but their service policy does not include reading magazines over the phone and I doubted if they would deliver at that hour, especially through a mail slot. I called George but he just laughed when he heard my voice and then hung up. I called my parents and my father said if I wasn't home in five minutes he'd call the police to come get me; I did not tell him where I was.

Then I called the publisher of *Uncanny Detective Stories* in New York, then the editor, then the managing editor, right on down the masthead. But the offices were closed and they all had unlisted phones. I didn't try Lester Swadding; I know a pen name when I see it, and I knew his phone would not be listed.

Then, admittedly, I got a little nervous and made a few trans-Atlantic calls. Scotland Yard never heard of McGronskey or Harberson. Oddly enough, there is an André Gennaud in Blackamoor Jail but he's in for forgery and he doesn't speak English.

I calmed down after that and read the rest óf the stories in the magazine which George had, ironically, left intact. Now I'm not really worried at all. I've got until Monday to get out and sooner or later I'll get in touch with someone who's read the story. I just hope McGronskey doesn't have a tricky ending up his sleeve. I hate tricky endings.

When Buying a Fine Murder
Jack Ritchie

DURING THE COURSE of the last twenty years I have been hired to kill quite a number of people and I have managed my missions with dispatch, neatness, and no subsequent embarrassment to my clients.

My victims have been varied in station and occupation, but they had at least one thing in common—an enemy who was willing to spend money for their demise.

This, however, was the first time someone had ever attempted to hire me to kill myself.

It wasn't that Walter Brandt *knew* he was engaging me to dispose of myself. He just knew that he was employing *someone* to do the job.

Obviously my relations with my clients must be circuitous. I cannot let anyone know just who I am and so I have a box number under an assumed name and communicate with my customers through that medium. And as an added precaution, I pick up my mail at odd hours, most often from midnight to morning.

I had no idea how Walter discovered the existence of my box, but I imagined that one of my former clients might have recommended me.

All this, of course, left me a little shaken and obviously reluctant.

I really didn't know Walter Brandt at all. He was, as a matter of fact, just someone I merely nod to at the club and I couldn't—for the life of me—imagine what possible reason he could have for wanting to bring about my death. Like most of my clients, he refused to divulge his motive. He simply wanted me out of this world.

And what was particularly crushing to my ego was that

Brandt was haggling about the price. We had exchanged three letters and so far we could come to no agreement. I would have declined the whole assignment, except, under the circumstances, I did not want Brandt to go to someone else with his commission.

I had to know more about Brandt and so one evening I managed the coincidence which put us in adjacent chairs before the club fireplace.

Brandt was a thin man, in his early forties, and the line of his profile was more or less diminuendo.

"Bit cold outside," I ventured. "Rather unusual for this time of year."

He drew his eyes away from his newspaper for a moment. "I hadn't noticed."

I listened to the fireplace logs crackle for half a minute. "I understand that you were once stalked by the giant sloth of South America."

He glanced up again. "That was Williams. However, most authorities consider the giant sloths to have been extinct long, long ago."

I nodded. "I've always been a bit dubious about Williams and his stories."

"Wouldn't mention it to Williams though," Brandt said. "He loses his temper easily. Killed a man once in Guatemala."

I doubted that too, but I took the opening. "Horrible thing to kill a man."

Brandt considered that. "Depends on the circumstances, I suppose."

"But surely if a man needs killing we must leave that job to society itself. We have courts, and juries, and . . ." I hesitated a moment. "And authorized executioners."

Brandt smiled faintly. "I often wonder if we have judges, juries, and executioners merely because we are cowards. We are afraid to do what must be done ourselves. We want to subdivide our feelings of guilt when we punish anyone."

Perhaps it was my imagination, but when he used the word "subdivide" something seemed to flicker in his eyes.

I probed further. "I simply can't understand any reason sufficiently important for one man to kill another."

Brandt raised an eyebrow. "For revenge. For a woman. For money. My dear man, there are hundreds of reasons."

Yes, I agreed silently, *there are hundreds of reasons. But what is yours? We are practically strangers, and yet you want to kill me.*

When I looked Brandt's way again, he was on the crossword puzzle and that clearly ended our conversation.

As I prepared to leave the club ten minutes later, Madsen helped me with my coat in the hall.

"This Walter Brandt," I said. "Nice chap."

"Yes, sir," Madsen said noncommittally.

"He's in railroads?"

Madsen straightened my collar. "No, sir. He's Brandt Enterprises. Apartment buildings."

It was nine-thirty when I got into the taxi for the ride home to my apartment and to my wife.

When one speaks of Helen, one inevitably feels compelled to add, "What a gorgeous creature," for she is near perfection in human form.

Have you ever noticed that a plain woman will develop her personality, or perhaps in extreme cases, her intelligence?

A beautiful woman feels no such compulsion. She just *is* and that is sufficient for her.

Helen can refrain from reading even the daily newspapers for weeks at a time without the slightest evidence of pain. The day she graduated from high school, she closed her books and her eyes have remained innocent of any attempt to strain the mind.

She does, though, have an instinctive protective sense. She realizes that in matters of the intellect her best response is attentiveness, a smile, and liberal silence.

Mind you, I am not complaining. I have a deep distrust for women who exhibit intelligence. They remind me rather of forced plants. The entire idea is contrary to the laws of nature.

I consider Helen perfect the way she is. I also collect Van Goghs, black jade statuary, and Gobelin tapestries. I do not expect any of them to be scintillating conversationalists either.

I found Helen quite by accident a year ago while she was working as the cashier in a small restaurant and I immediately recognized that I had found a jewel destined for a setting.

Helen proved amenable—to a degree. I would have preferred a less binding arrangement, but the morals of Sheboygan were still fresh with her, and I found myself, at the age of forty-five, joining the ranks of the benedicts.

When I entered the apartment I found Helen before her dressing table.

"You're home early," she said, not taking her eyes from the mirror.

"I felt rather tired." I watched her gently massaging her face. "How much of the day does that take?"

She glanced up at my reflection. "About ten or fifteen minutes, I'd say."

"I mean the whole thing. All the grooming."

"Including the clothes?"

I sighed. "Yes. Including the clothes."

She appeared as thoughtful as she could. "I really don't know, Ronnie. But it keeps me busy all day. I hardly know where the time goes."

"Don't you ever get bored?"

She looked back over her shoulder. "Why no, Ronnie. There's always something to do. Like nails, or hair." Her eyes went back to the mirror. "Do you ever get bored, Ronnie?"

I was a bit startled. "Me? Of course not. No man of intellect does."

"I mean you just walk around and touch those wall carpets, or play with those little plastic statues or stare at those gloomy paintings. Doesn't that bore you?"

"Van Gogh was one of the world's greatest painters," I explained tolerantly.

"Really? How do you know?"

"The critics are in complete agreement."

"I mean do you *really* like him or do you think you ought to. To keep in style, I mean."

I was faintly irritated. "I am a man of impeccable taste."

"I know, Ronnie. Of course you are." She seemed to

examine me for a moment or two. "I never pried, Ronnie. I know you have an inheritance or something, because you never work. But I think you ought to do something. Something important, I mean. So you don't get bored."

"I am *not* bored."

"You ought to be able to feel as though you're important to the world."

It was difficult to keep my temper. "I *am* important to the world. You have no idea how important."

"Of course you're important to me," she said soothingly. "But I mean you should take up something important to your fellowman."

"Like what?" I demanded.

"Oh, I don't know, Ronnie. But something significant. Like life and death."

My temper dissipated and I smiled. "Perhaps some day, my dear."

She wiped her fingertips on tissue. "Ronnie, are you satisfied with me?"

I patted her shoulder. "I like you just the way you are. I wouldn't want anything changed."

She smiled. "That's what I thought."

I went into the living room, made myself a drink, and sat down to enjoy it.

I congratulated myself as I looked about the room. I was most fortunate in finding this apartment and during the course of ten years it had become my storehouse, the repository for my treasures.

The superintendent of the building had been hectoring me lately to give up my lease. He wanted to cut up the rooms to create three smaller apartments out of one. But I stood firmly on my rights. My lease was ironclad and extendible.

Our discussions became so heated, in fact, that one time I descended to the vernacular, "Over my dead body!"

Now I sipped my drink and this moment would have been perfect except that the problem of Walter Brandt again intruded itself into my mind.

Why in the world would he want to kill me? For money? He very likely had fifty times as much as I had. For revenge? Revenge of what? I'd never harmed him in any possible way I could imagine.

For a woman?

I was about to shake my head to that too when a staggering speculation came to me.

But it was preposterous! Ridiculous!

And yet . . . ?

I was absolutely certain of Helen. Besides she hadn't the imagination for anything like . . . I treat her well, I thought peevishly. She wants for nothing.

It was too tenuous, too impossible to consider.

I found myself breathing rather hard.

Helen and Brandt? My mind seemed to squeak. Amour? With Walter Brandt?

But he was so . . . so insignificant. Really not cultured at all. Hardly presentable physically.

Yet women are notoriously unpredictable in their choices of . . . companions.

The next morning I left the apartment early.

The agency I selected was a large one. I believe in patronizing the best, certainly the most successful, when one must resort to employing private detectives.

There was a quiet, soft-lighted waiting room and a receptionist whose voice was modulated and whose appearance showed tasteful grooming.

Mr. Lister, who apparently was in charge, had a gray military mustache and a Princeton class ring.

I was brief and to the point. "I would like to have my wife under surveillance."

Lister was businesslike. "Do you suspect anything?"

"I merely want my wife watched. I believe that should be sufficient for your purposes."

"Of course," Lister said equably. "Do you desire any particular portion of the day?"

"Twenty-four hours."

He nodded. "I merely asked because some of our clients like to save money. They usually prefer to take over one eight-hour shift for themselves."

He studied my clothes and appeared satisfied. "I will have the men on eight-hour shifts. However, since they do not work seven days a week, it will be necessary to hire an additional three men on weekends."

"As many men as you need," I said.

"Would you like the reports weekly?"

"Daily. I'll pick them up myself."

When I left him, he was happily computing figures on his desk pad.

I spent several hours at an art gallery, a boorish regional exhibition, and then, finding myself in the neighborhood of the restaurant where I'd discovered Helen, I followed a whim and entered.

The waitress who came to my table smiled brightly. "Why, Mr. Reynolds. Imagine seeing you here again."

"I'm sorry, but . . ."

"Oh, I don't expect you to remember me. I never waited on you here and we were introduced only once. That was at Helen's wedding."

"But, of course," I said. However as far as I was concerned, her birdlike features were completely unfamiliar.

"I'm Elsie Schwendt," she said and then giggled. "I mean Elsie Barrows. It's so hard to get used to, to my new name."

"I imagine so. I would like a rare sirloin."

She pointed to a tense-faced man who was evidently lecturing a bus boy. "That's Mr. Barrows. We were married just two months ago. He's the assistant manager and he wants me to work as long as I can, but—"

"Yes," I said. "And sliced tomatoes."

"Someday I intend to look Helen up and see how she's doing."

"By all means. Just the steak and tomatoes. No side dishes or bread."

"Helen and I came east at the same time," she said, "and got jobs here. I was one of her girlfriends in high school." She felt impelled to qualify that. "Not one of her really close friends though. She was more the intellectual type and read a lot."

I chuckled. "Helen? Intellectual?"

Elsie Barrows nodded. "She was valedictorian of her graduating class."

I laughed shortly. "How many were there in the class? Three? Four?"

"Why, no," Elsie said. "There were 326 students who graduated. And Helen had the highest average in the history of the school."

I took a sip of water and smiled. "My dear Mrs. Barrows, are we talking about the same person? My wife is Helen Thorne Reynolds."

"Of course," Elsie said. "Thorne was her maiden name."

I rubbed my chin and scowled.

"I suppose she attends classes during the day," Elsie said.

"Classes? What classes?"

"College, of course."

I was getting warm and irritated. "I'm afraid I don't know what you're talking about."

Elsie seemed surprised. "Isn't Helen going to college?"

My patience was frayed almost beyond endurance. "My dear Mrs. Barrows, Helen is not going to college."

Elsie digested the information. "That's strange. Helen always said she wanted a college education more than anything else. That and money, of course. All of us girls were very sensible about wanting money."

She gazed fondly in the direction of her husband. "I passed up a lot of opportunities until I found Henry. He's only twenty-six and already assistant manager here. This restaurant is one of a chain, you know." Her face was proud. "Henry will go far. He's an Organization Man."

I realized I was making water rings on the tablecloth and stopped. "There's a Cheboygan in Michigan. Perhaps you're getting it confused with . . ."

"Sheboygan. In Wisconsin," Elsie said. "Helen's folks couldn't afford to send her to college and so she came to New York to earn money. She was going to work a year, then go to college a year, and then work another year and so on until she got all the way up to her doctor's degree. Mathematics, I think."

Elsie regarded me with the coyness of a possible secret. "Are you sure Helen isn't going to college?"

"I wouldn't allow her to," I snapped.

"I mean maybe when you're working and away from home."

"I do not work," I said stiffly. "I am home most of the time and I have never noticed Helen either going to or returning from college."

"That's funny," Elsie said. "Helen always said she wanted to go to college more than anything else in the world. And Helen always got what she wanted." She reflected a moment. "You know, Helen once told me that she'd kill anybody who tried to stop her from getting one. I think she meant it too."

That was the last straw. "Oh, come now! People just don't go about killing people in order to go to college."

"I guess not," Elsie admitted. "But still sometimes when Helen wanted something and she couldn't get it . . ." Elsie shivered a little. "Helen has very funny eyes. Have you noticed? Sort of green and sometimes they seem to glow. But then the whole family was a little . . ." She stopped and blushed. "Be sure to give my regards to Helen. Sirloin rare and tomatoes?"

The steak was overdone, as seems to be the usual case, and the cut was more Utility than Prime.

As I was paying for my dinner, a piece of paper fell out of my wallet. I picked it up and glanced at it idly. It was a receipt for my last month's rent and I noticed something that had escaped my attention before.

The printed heading on the receipt indicated that I'd been paying my rent to Brandt Enterprises. It was something that I'd never realized before, since all my dealings were with the superintendent.

An amusing thought occurred to me. Suppose Brandt were actually trying to get rid of me because I refused to allow my apartment to be subdivided.

It was something to titillate the mind.

The cashier was looking at me rather peculiarly and I realized that I'd been chuckling. "Just remembering a joke I heard earlier today," I explained hastily.

In the hall of my apartment, I took off my hat and coat and stood in front of the mirror to adjust my personal appearance.

I saw that the mirror reflected a portion of the living room mirror and that in turn revealed a corner of the room. Idly I experimented a bit by moving from side to side until the entire living room came into view.

Helen was in an easy chair.

And she was reading a book!

More than that, she had a pencil in her hand and a pad of paper on her knee. Every few moments she would frown and scribble something on the pad.

I steadied myself against a small table, and that toppled a vase of flowers.

Helen's movements were feline swift and I watched, fascinated. In a moment the book, the pad, and the pencil disappeared beneath the cushions of her chair and Helen became something languid, serene, placidly unoccupied.

"Is that you, dear?" she called.

I pulled myself together. "Yes, Helen."

Later that evening, when she was out of the room, I investigated beneath the cushions. I recognized only one of the equations on the pad of paper. It was one of the few things I remembered from my required Mathematical Analysis course in college.

The next three weeks were entirely unsatisfactory. Brandt continued to haggle about the price of my death and, despite my proddings, persistently refused to divulge his motive.

And Helen went well into integral calculus.

In Mr. Lister's office, I finished reading his twenty-first daily report and put it aside. "Nothing. Absolutely nothing."

"Nothing at all suspicious," Lister agreed. "She's seen no one whom we might construe as a . . . rival."

"Not even college," I muttered. "Either she's taking correspondence lessons or she's doing this on her own."

Lister raised an eyebrow. "College?"

"Nothing." I sighed. "I think it would be useless to watch her any further."

Lister agreed, but reluctantly. "Usually if they have been seeing someone, they just can't bear to keep apart for more than a week. You have a completely faithful wife, Mr. Reynolds."

He studied me a moment and then cleared his throat. "However, if you desired, I'm sure we could arrange something that would hold up in any court."

I scowled at him.

Lister shrugged. "Just a thought."

That evening I was hardly aware of the Beethoven concerto on my record player as I sat and brooded. Brandt's motive remained a mystery. Except for the wretched possibility that he wanted my apartment so badly that . . .

No. Such a thought was hardly worthy of consideration. And Helen.

Naturally I was relieved that she was completely faithful, but those secret studies would have to stop. I would have to speak to her soon.

"Would you like a drink, dear?" Helen asked.

I came out of my reverie. "Thank you, my dear." I got to my feet. "I'll be back in a moment. I'd like to change to my smoking jacket."

I selected the maroon silk from the bedroom closet and prepared to rejoin Helen. In the hall I automatically stopped to look in the mirror. I had been doing that for the last three weeks, often profitably.

I saw Helen put two drinks on the cocktail table. I was about to turn away and enter the living room, when something stopped me.

Helen had a small white envelope in her hand and she tore off a corner.

I watched with increasing fascination as she carefully tapped the contents into the glass that was intended for me. When the envelope was evidently empty, she crumpled it into a tiny ball and dropped it into an ashtray.

Then she resumed her chair and smiled. It was a slow, waiting smile.

I wiped my moist fingers and strolled into the living room.

Helen's face was smoothed of expression, but her eyes appeared rather more attentive than her features indicated. "The drinks are ready, dear."

"Thank you. Your martinis are always perfect." While I lit a cigarette I let my eyes stray to the glass. The powder was undetectable. "Had a busy day, dear?"

"About like usual, Ronnie."

I still felt shaken. It was insane. Irrational. One simply does not kill one's husband just because one wants to go to college.

I licked my lips. "My dear, I'm beginning to think that perhaps I've been a bit selfish."

She showed faint surprise. "Selfish?"

"Yes, my dear. Here I have kept you secluded as something of a jewel, a thing of beauty."

Only the corners of her mouth indicated a smile. "You've treated me well, Ronnie."

"Yes," I agreed. "But I have never considered that you might be more than a woman, an ornament; that you might have a mind too and that you'd like to give it some license." I corrected that. "Some expression."

I plunged into the cold water. "Have you ever thought about going to college?"

Her eyes flickered. "Whatever gave you that idea?"

"It was just something that came to my mind." I was perspiring slightly. "Why don't you enroll? Tomorrow. Or whenever the semester starts?"

Her smile was languid. "Why, thank you, Ronnie."

"Then you will?"

"I'll think it over." Then her voice became a shade commanding. "Try your drink, Ronnie."

I was aghast. Here I had just given her blanket permission to go to college and yet she still wanted to kill me!

And then, in a flash, reason returned to me.

Of course! I had been thinking like a panicky fool. How ridiculous one's thoughts become in a moment of stress.

Helen wanted to kill me for the simplest and most classic of reasons. She wanted to get rid of me so she could have my money.

I felt somewhat giddy with elation. The world was logical again. Sane. Rational.

I almost drank to that before I remembered the contents of my glass.

And it was all so amusing. I lived well, but I lived on my income. I had no capital and, at the moment, I was worth less than three thousand dollars.

I suppose it wouldn't have been at all difficult to distract her attenion for a moment and switch drinks. But I put the thought aside. It would put me in an embarrassing position. I had no plans for the disposal of her body and improvising in such a situation is a tricky business.

Helen leaned forward and picked up her drink. Her action was plainly intended to prompt me and I complied.

I sniffed the frosted glass and was faintly disappointed not to detect the odor of almonds. "Helen," I said. "Have you been happy with me?"

"Of course, dear." She sipped her drink and waited for me to emulate her.

I put the glass to my lips for a moment and then lowered it without tasting the martini. "And I with you, my dear."

Perhaps "contented" would have been a more accurate word. After our marriage I enjoyed the same feeling of accomplishment and satisfaction. I'd experienced when I acquired one of the Arles landscapes.

Helen's eyes were on my glass.

I laughed slightly. "You know, Helen, I was forty-five when I married you and I'd been a bachelor for a long time."

She seemed to take a deeper breath than usual. "Yes, dear. For forty-five years. Your drink is getting warm."

"And naturally, being single for so long, one tends to become set in one's ways—to form certain reservations on all matters—to become . . . ah, suspicious."

Her eyes narrowed. "Suspicious?"

I made my smile as disarming as I could. "After all, there you were, a beautiful young woman who certainly could have done better. And there was I, a man of forty-five." I cleared my throat. "With money."

There was a definite greenish glow in Helen's eyes.

I raised the glass to my lips, hesitated a moment, and then put it down again, untasted.

I am positive the mind of Helen Thorne Reynolds swore.

"And so," I said. "I never did get around to changing my will."

Helen's head cocked slowly. "Will?"

I nodded. "You see I leave everything to my brother."

Actually I have no brother. No will either, for that matter.

"But now that some time has passed and we've become so adjusted, so happy, I intend to change it." I smiled benignly. "I am going to make you my sole beneficiary the next time I see my lawyer."

I picked up the drink and raised it to my lips. "Well, cheers."

It was surprising how fast Helen moved. One moment in an easy chair six feet away and the next standing beside me with her fingers firmly about my glass.

"Your drink is much too warm. I'll pour you another."

We played fingertip tug-of-war. "No, my dear. I really prefer martinis this way. I get the full flavor."

"Nonsense," she said positively. "The reason martinis are chilled is to kill the taste. Otherwise they remind you of gasoline."

What Helen did next was not original. However, under the circumstances, action was more imperative than originality and the glass shot from my hand and tumbled to the rug.

"Oh, dear," Helen said routinely. "How clumsy of me. I do hope I haven't ruined the rug."

"Never mind the rug, dear," I said soothingly. "I'm sure the spot can be removed."

Helen brought me another martini. It was chilled and delicious. As I drank, I reflected sadly that now I would have to get rid of Helen before she got rid of me.

It was slightly after five the next afternoon and Helen was still at her hairdresser's, when the buzzer of my apartment sounded.

When I opened the door, Walter Brandt stood in front of me.

The static of alarm alerted my body. Perhaps Brandt, quibbling soul that he was, had decided to save money and dispose of me himself.

"Mr. Reynolds," he said diffidently. "May I speak with you for a few moments?"

I believe I would have closed the door in his face except that Millie, our cook, took that moment to leave our apartment for the day.

"I'm going home now, Mr. Reynolds," she said.

It swiftly occurred to me that Brandt would not be foolish enough to murder me after he had been identified to a potential witness. A murderer just doesn't do that. At least I never have.

"Millie," I said. "This is Mr. Walter Brandt. He is Brandt Enterprises. The owner of this building."

They were mutually surprised by the introduction.

Millie opened her mouth to supply her last name, something which I had purposely omitted.

"Now run along, Millie, and be sure to tell all your friends that you met Walter Brandt at . . . ," I glanced at my watch. "Precisely 5:17."

I watched her go and then rubbed my hands. "Won't you come in, Mr. Brandt?"

Five minutes later we were seated in my study and Brandt smiled in the manner of a man about to shock someone.

"Mr. Reynolds," he said. "For the last five weeks I have been negotiating with a man to kill you."

The gall of the man! To come right out and admit it! He held up a hand. "Rest easy, Mr. Reynolds. The negotiations haven't been completed yet."

"Good," I said emphatically.

His smile widened. "I think I'd better start at the beginning. Do you remember Clement Hudson?"

I did. He had been one of my clients. But I was cautious. "No."

Brandt supplied information. "Two years ago Hudson's wife was murdered. At first the police suspected Hudson. It seems that everyone knew that he and she had been quarreling bitterly. She had the money in the family and gave him nothing more than a pitiful allowance."

I caught myself nodding and stopped.

"But Hudson had an unbreakable alibi. He was in the

presence of at least fifteen people and over two hundred miles away when the murder was committed."

Of course, I thought complacently. *It was planned that way.*

"The whole affair struck Hudson extremely hard," Brandt said. "He became utterly despondent."

Remorseful, I corrected mentally.

"I was in his apartment when it happened," Brandt said.

I sat up. "His wife's murder?"

"No. When Hudson killed himself."

"Oh," I said with some relief.

"I was his best friend. I had been trying to console him over the loss of his wife, but apparently there was nothing I could do." Brandt shook his head sadly. "It happened so suddenly Hudson left the room. I thought he was just getting his coat to go for a walk, but then I heard the shot. I rushed into his bedroom and there he was, on the floor. It was ghastly."

"That's the way it goes," I said. "He was dead?"

Brandt smiled significantly. "No. Not quite."

I stirred uneasily.

"He died within a matter of seconds, but before he did, he whispered something to me." Brandt's voice became a dramatic whisper. "He said, 'I killed her.' "

"But obviously that was impossible."

"That's not all he said. He also whispered a number. '1217.' "

I felt cold. That was my box number at the post office. "Are you positive?"

"Absolutely. I have very good hearing."

"Anything else?" I asked warily.

"Nothing. Just that. 'I killed her. 1217.' "

I decided to make myself a drink. "You told the police?"

Brandt shook his head. "No. As I told you, Hudson was my best friend. At the time I felt positive that he couldn't have killed his wife. I felt that his last words were a delirium, possibly expressing simply a feeling of guilt that he hadn't been there to protect his wife. Under those circumstances, I saw no reason to tell the police. It would simply have jeopardized the good name of my friend.

One of his phrases seemed to stick out and I repeated it. "At the time?"

Brandt nodded. "At the time I thought Hudson couldn't have killed his wife, but then about a year ago the thought came to me that perhaps Hudson really had been responsible for her death. He could have *hired* someone to kill her."

What a keen, swift mind, I thought wryly. It took you only a year to think of that. "And *then* you went to the police?"

Brandt flushed slightly. "No. It had been over a year since Hudson killed himself, and I was afraid that the police might interpret my silence as obstructing justice."

"A distinct possibility," I murmured.

"And the number 1217 kept nagging at my mind until one day while I was collecting my mail, it suddenly struck me. 1217 could be the number of a postal box."

I put very little soda in my glass and took a swallow. Then I remembered my manners and began making a drink for Brandt.

"Then I thought further," Brandt said. "If Hudson had actually employed a killer, couldn't the negotiations have been conducted by mail through box number 1217?"

"And *then*, of course, you went to the police?"

Brandt flushed again. "No. By this time eighteen months had passed. I would have been in more trouble than before."

And these are the very people who complain about police inaction in murder cases, I reflected sadly.

Brandt took a breath. "But I couldn't just leave everything there and forget about it. So I decided to try an experiment. I addressed a letter to the box myself—to negotiate for a murder."

I handed him his drink and said nothing.

"I was right," Brandt said with considerable elation. "It was the box number of a man who could be hired to kill."

I pursed my lips. "And why, pray, did you select me as your victim?"

Brandt smiled. "I really haven't an enemy in the world. And so while I was pondering on who to select as my victim, I was stumped until your name suddenly came to mind."

"I don't even know you," I said testily. "I've never harmed you in my life."

Brandt chuckled. "Not in a major way. But you've been giving Brandt Enterprises a little trouble. I'm converting this building into smaller apartments and so far everyone has willingly come to an agreement to vacate—except you."

"Just because a man won't give up his apartment is no sane reason to resort to murder," I said indignantly. "That's the most cold-blooded, inhuman thing I've ever heard of."

"Tut, tut," Brandt said soothingly. "Of course I had no intention of actually going through with it."

"Well! I should hope not!"

"I merely wanted to engage in correspondence with him. I intended to watch the box and see who picked up the mail." Brandt shook his head. "Unfortunately my plan isn't working."

I barely concealed my pleasure and relief. "Really?"

"I can't watch the box twenty-four hours a day. It is physically impossible and besides I have a great deal of other work to do. The best I could manage was my lunch period and a few hours in the evening. But he never collected his mail while I was there." Brandt sighed. "I prolonged the correspondence by pretending to haggle about the price, but . . . ." He shrugged.

I felt generous at his failure.

"The police could have the box watched twenty-four hours a day."

"No," Brandt said wearily. "I told you that it would be too embarrassing to explain everything to them now. And besides, suppose something goes wrong? If the killer got suspicious and abandoned the box, I would find myself in a great deal of additional trouble with the authorities."

My drink was delicious. "And so you have failed?"

He nodded grudgingly. "So far." Then his expression warned me that he was about to enjoy startling me again. "I have decided to bring matters to a head. I will agree to his price and tell him to go ahead and kill you."

"My dear man . . ." I began patiently.

"Naturally I won't actually allow him to go through with it."

"I should hope not."

"He wants fifteen thousand and I will pay it," Brandt said. "Though I think that's a rather high figure."

"It all depends on one's point of view."

"I will insist on certain specifications. I will direct the time you are to be murdered and the place." He looked about. "Right here in your study seems ideal."

"Yes," I agreed. "It is comfortable."

Brandt obviously had already made the plans. "You will arrange to be alone on the chosen night. You will be here in your study. At eight-thirty the murderer will let himself into your apartment and creep up behind you."

"You will provide him with a key?"

"If I may borrow one of yours?"

"Of course."

"He will steal into the study and strike you over the head."

"Frankly, I'd prefer to be shot."

"No. I will insist that you be struck over the head. If the killer used a gun, the whole thing might be over before I can spring from my hiding place."

"Ah, you will spring from your hiding place?"

Brandt nodded. "The moment he raises the lethal weapon to strike. I will leap out with my revolver and catch him in the act. *Flagrante delicto.* You do have a closet or something like that where I can conceal myself?"

"Yes. That door over there."

He leaned forward eagerly. "Then you agree?"

The whole adventure obviously was going to fail. Still, it was an opportunity to pick up fifteen thousand dollars. "Very well," I said. "You may make the arrangements."

During the next week, Brandt and Box Number 1217 brought their negotiations to a conclusion. I insisted upon and received the fifteen thousand dollars in advance, my usual procedure, and this time I took the additional precaution of specifying small bills.

I reasoned that if they were large, Brandt might take

the trouble to make a list of the serial numbers and they might eventually be placed into the efficient hands of the police.

Brandt selected a Tuesday evening and he arrived at my apartment at seven.

That was the correct time.

I led him into the study. "I thought you'd never get here."

He glanced at his watch. "I'm precisely on time."

I looked at my own watch and then let my eyes wander to the electric wall clock and then to the grandfather clock in the corner. "Your watch is half an hour slow."

The evidence was arranged and overwhelming. Brandt put his watch ahead a half an hour. "Are you alone?"

"No. My wife's still here."

Brandt protested. "But . . ."

"She'll be leaving in a few moments. She's going to a movie and won't be back until eleven or threereabouts. Everything should be over by then. Are you armed?"

Brandt took the .38 caliber revolver from his pocket. He was obviously uneasy about handling it. "This belonged to my father."

I heard Helen in the hall and opened the door of my study. She was putting on her gloves.

"Oh, by the way, Helen," I said. "This is Walter Brandt."

Brandt came into her view behind me. He blinked as he looked at her.

She nodded. "A pleasure."

"We'll be busy in here for quite awhile, Helen," I said. "Good-bye, my dear." I closed the door and Brandt and I were alone again.

"What a gorgeous creature," Brandt whispered almost to himself. Then he came out of his daze and went to the closet door. He disappeared inside for a moment and then returned. "I'll leave the door open about one inch. That way I can see you at the desk and the door behind you."

"Don't take your eyes off me for a second," I said.

"Of course not. Your life is in my hands."

"Yes. I suppose it is. Would you care for a drink? It will help us relax. We really can't expect the murderer for another hour and there's no sense in you crouching in the closet for that long."

At the liquor cabinet I had my back to him when I tapped the grayish powder into his glass. I had measured it previously to suit a man of his general build and weight. I stirred both drinks and brought him his. "Now sit down and enjoy this."

Brandt was reluctant and I practically had to force him into the easy chair. It wasn't that I was concerned for his comfort. I simply didn't want him to fall forward and perhaps bruise his face. That might be difficult to explain.

"Bottoms up," I said and watched him down about half his glass. "I've told a number of people that you would be here."

Brandt was startled. "Why do that?"

"Just a precaution," I said. "But I haven't told them why you're here." I thought I'd make things unmistakably clear. "The thought struck me that you might actually want to murder me after all."

His eyes widened. "That's absurd."

"Yes," I said. "I suppose it is. But if you had intended to murder me, what better opportunity than under the arrangements you made. I would be alone and unsuspecting."

He laughed shortly. "Your wife knows I'm here."

"But I arranged that myself."

"Then why bother telling other people I'd be here?"

I smiled. "Perhaps my wife wouldn't remember." What I meant was that she might not want to remember. I am a very, very cautious man. There still might be some connection between the two of them. Something I hadn't been able to discover.

Brandt shook his head. "Why would I pay fifteen thousand dollars to hire a killer if I intended to murder you myself?"

"You might be squeamish about performing the actual job. He would do that. You would simply fail to warn me when he entered the room."

Brandt finished his drink. "You are remarkably suspicious."

"Yes," I said. "And foresighted." I glanced at my watch. It would take approximately five to six minutes for the powder in his drink to take effect. "A cigarette, Mr. Brandt?"

"I don't usually."

"But this time is an exception," I insisted.

I filled the minutes by going over our plans again and I watched Brandt carefully.

It happened suddenly, as it was supposed to do. His eyes closed and I caught the cigarette as it fell from his fingers.

I tamped it out, broke it, and scattered the tobacco in the wastebasket.

Then I went into the hall to wait.

Helen was not at a movie.

Just before I expected Brandt I had explained to her that I desperately needed some aspirins. We were completely out—something which I had arranged—and would she please go to the drugstore and fetch me some. I would go myself except that I expected a visitor at any moment.

I had timed the errand previously.

Descending in the elevator, walking to the drugstore, making the purchase, and returning was an operation that averaged twenty minutes.

Helen was not dilatory, one of her virtues, and I expected her back promptly. Nevertheless, I breathed a sigh of relief when I heard her key in the lock.

She closed the door behind her. "Is your friend still here?"

"Yes, in the study."

I examined her face for the last time. It was such a pity to be forced to destroy a thing of beauty.

She was putting her purse and gloves on the table when I picked up the solid brass ashtray and struck.

It was swift and complete and she made no sound as she dropped to the floor. I made certain that she was dead; then I wiped the ashtray and placed it beside her.

I then rejoined Brandt in the study.

He did have the appearance of being dead, a fact which caused me a moment of apprehension, but a check proved he was quite alive, though still unconscious.

If my calculations proved correct, and I was certain they were, he would wake up in about fifteen minutes—a total sleep of one half hour.

I reset both clocks, my wrist watch, and Brandt's back one half hour to the correct time.

Then I watched him and waited. When I was certain he was on the brink of consciousness, I broke a cigarette in half and lighted one of the pieces. I put it on the lip of the ashtray next to him.

The process of returning to consciousness could take a drowsy minute or two, but I wanted to make it sharp. I slapped a heavy book on one corner of my desk.

". . . certainly a lot more comfortable," I said clearly and loudly.

Brandt blinked. "What?"

"I said that it would certainly be a lot more comfortable if you took a chair into the closet."

Brandt glanced at the wall clocks and checked his wrist watch. His eyes noted the cigarette still burning on the tray and his rational mind told him that if he had dropped off it had been for only a second or two. More likely his attention had just wandered.

And so a half-hour was born and died and Brandt was unaware of it.

"Now one thing," I said. "You mustn't fall asleep."

Brandt stifled a yawn. "Of course not."

I smiled. "I just mean that your eyes must never leave me."

"You can depend on me," Brandt said firmly.

The next three hours were interminable. I sat at my desk reading a detective novel. Normally I enjoy them, but this time I was greatly relieved when Brandt finally came out of the closet at eleven o'clock.

"I don't understand what went wrong," he complained petulantly.

"You never should have paid in advance," I admonished. "Your killer simply pocketed the money and decided not to risk the actual murder."

And then we found Helen's body in the hall.

Naturally the police suspected me. But how could I

possibly have committed the murder? I had been in Brandt's presence when I had last seen my wife and I had never left his sight until we found her body.

Poor Brandt had a miserable time with the police. They were extremely skeptical about our waiting for a hired killer to appear, but in the end, there was no other explanation.

Helen had decided not to go to the movies or perhaps she had forgotten something and returned to our apartment.

Either she had surprised the killer in the hall, or he had entered moments after she did. He had killed her to prevent recognition or an outcry and then fled.

I regretted losing Helen. She was so beautiful, so ravishing. Especially when she stood against the tapestry with the hunting motif.

But I did have the fifteen thousand dollars.

And there was one other pleasant thing. Brandt Enterprises never again badgered me about subdividing my apartment.